THE MOST UNEQUAL CONTEST

Lord Cleveland was the most sought-after prize in the London marriage mart. He was wonderfully good-looking, wealthy, intelligent, honorable, and kind. He also made it plain that he adored Miss Dilys Bryn and wanted to make her his bride.

Lord Gallant, on the other hand, was a man whom proper mothers made their daughters assiduously avoid—for since the devilishly handsome Gallant could have any woman he wanted, whenever he wanted her, it had become clear that marriage was not on his mind.

It should have been no contest when Dilys had to choose between these two. And it wasn't one. For this incurably romantic young lady unhesitatingly followed her heart on a path that others might consider wickedly wrong . . . but to Dilys was gloriously right. . . .

NORMA LEE CLARK was born in Joplin, Missouri, but considers herself a New Yorker, having lived in Manhattan longer than in her native state. In addition to writing Regencies, she is also the private secretary to Woody Allen.

FP

The Infamous Rake

by

Norma Lee Clark

A SIGNET BOOK

NEW AMERICAN LIBRARY

A DIVISION OF PENGUIN BOOKS USA INC.

NAL BOOKS ARE AVAILABLE AT QUANTITY DISCOUNTS WHEN USED TO
PROMOTE PRODUCTS OR SERVICES. FOR INFORMATION PLEASE WRITE
TO PREMIUM MARKETING DIVISION, NEW AMERICAN LIBRARY,
1633 BROADWAY, NEW YORK, NEW YORK 10019.

SIGNET TRADEMARK REG.U.S. PAT. OFF. AND FOREIGN COUNTRIES
REGISTERED TRADEMARK—MARCA REGISTRADA
HECHO EN DRESDEN, TN., U.S.A.

SIGNET, SIGNET CLASSIC, MENTOR, ONYX, PLUME, MERIDIAN and
NAL BOOKS are published by New American Library, a division of Penguin
Books USA Inc., 1633 Broadway, New York, New York 10010

First Printing, February, 1990

1 2 3 4 5 6 7 8 9

PRINTED IN THE UNITED STATES OF AMERICA

1

Today we did sums and Mlle said I was making some progress. I did feel somehow more easy while doing them than I ever have before, though I fear I shall never become proficient in them. Then Mlle had the headache and I went to look for Georgeanne and she was in the back drawing room with Travis and he was telling her she was a coldhearted flirt and she was laughing at him. He looked so furious, his eyebrows drawn together and his black eyes shooting sparks. He looked like Lucifer! And then I realized he was the handsomest man I had ever seen in all my life. I wonder how Georgeanne can resist him?

This was only part of the entry in Dilys' diary for that day. She always wrote fulsomely, for there was a great deal of time at her disposal despite the lessons from Mlle she was subject to. Today's entry was somewhat more interesting than her usual efforts, comprising, as they mostly did, lists of the lessons she had had and what she had been given for dinner. Lord Travis Gallant had figured in her entries before, but in a much more offhand fashion. He was a cousin, and she had known him all the eight years of her life, but only today had taken in the fact that he was exceedingly handsome and become shy in his presence.

When she told Mlle over their dinner in the nursery that Lord Travis looked like Lucifer, Mlle told her repressively not to be blasphemous and to get on with her meal. Dilys subsided obediently, aware that Mlle must still be suffering with the headache, since ordinarily she was more than willing to discuss anyone with a title.

Undismayed by this snub, Dilys put the same proposition to Georgeanne that same night as she sat in her dressing room on the end of Georgeanne's bed.

"Lucifer! Well—yes, I suppose in a way," responded Georgeanne, deftly plaiting her waist-length tresses as she sat up against her pillows. "Beautiful as the angel of darkness—and all that."

"Then how can you resist him when he is so much in love with you?"

"In love? Pooh, Dilly, you know nothing about anything if you call that love," Georgeanne replied, tossing her head contemptuously. "He's only a boy, barely out of leading strings."

"He is eighteen the same as you."

"Yes, but everyone knows that boys of eighteen are only boys still, while girls of eighteen are women. If we were both twenty-five, I might give more credence to his declarations. But then, if that were the case he would not be making them! I would be a spinster by then and he would not consider me but go looking for a girl of eighteen."

"Then may women of five-and-twenty never marry?"

"Oh, yes, of course they may, but by then they must make the best of things and take who ever asks them and consider themselves lucky."

"I could never do that! Why, the man may be a—a monster! I could never marry a man I did not love just to be married. I should sooner be a spinster all my life."

"Easy to say that now when you are only eight years old and just discovering romance," Georgeanne said, "but a whole different proposition when you are five-and-twenty and life is passing you by and everyone is looking upon you pityingly because you have had no offers. Besides, women sometimes fall in love with monsters and marry them before they discover their mistake.''

"What is all this unsuitable talk of monsters just at bedtime, Lady Georgeanne?'' said Mlle sternly from the doorway. "Is it your wish to cause the child to have nightmares? Come along now, Miss Dilys. You should have been in your bed this half-hour ago.''

Dilys kissed Georgeanne and went away with Mlle. She was never inclined to be disobedient in any case, and besides, she had a great deal to think of. When her bedroom door closed firmly behind Mlle, she rose, lit her candle again, and proceeded to record her entire conversation with Georgeanne in her diary so she would not forget any of it.

It was by any standards an unusual conversation between an eighteen-year-old and a child of eight, but their circumstances made it less so. Dilys Bryn had been an orphan from birth. Her father, Lord Walter Bryn, a Welsh coal-mine baron, broke his neck on the hunting field the day before Dilys' birth. The shock had brought Lady Bryn to an untimely lying-in and her difficulties there had caused her to expire just as Dilys drew her first breath and began to wail.

Dilys' aunt, her mother's sister, Lady Langthorne, had immediately adopted the child and brought her home to be raised as a sister to Georgeanne, her only child. Georgeanne at ten had made Dilys her own special charge. She hung over her cradle by the hour prattling away, helped Nanny bathe and change her, taught her to walk, and when she was toddling, played endless games with her. For eight years she had confided her inmost secrets to Dilys, never doubting her secrets were safe even when, quite early on, she found that Dilys understood a great deal more than she had given her credit for.

They were brought up as sisters by the Earl and Countess

of Langthorne, and Dilys had never felt that life had treated her shabbily. Apart from this loving family, she had a brother, Alun, but he being twelve at her birth and away at school, she barely knew him. His vacations had always been spent with his godfather, and Dilys had seen him only three times in her life so far. He was now two-and-twenty, a young man about town in London, where, according to Georgeanne, who had seen him frequently during her come-out there and in her one Season in London since, he lived a most exemplary life.

"Actually, a bit of a prig, Dilly dear, if you'll forgive my saying so. No vices, you know, and pompous with it. He has his eye on Caroline Dudham—you know the one I have told you about—swimming in money and no chin to speak of. Though why he should hang out for a wealthy wife *I* don't know. He surely has enough from your father to marry where he likes, and he cannot like Caro Dudham. Nobody does."

"Why?"

"Why what?"

"Why does no one like Caroline Dudham?"

"But I have told you. She is sour and mean to everyone—at least to everyone below her in station. Though what she has to be so high in the instep about confounds me. Her father is only a baron, after all, and the first in his line. Before that they were only squires and farmers until Lord Dudham made all that money importing cocoa or something."

Dilys found all this interesting enough to record in her diary. She had cared very little for her brother the few times she had met him. She knew Travis better and liked him a great deal more. Being her and Georgeanne's cousin, several times removed, he had been accustomed to visit quite frequently throughout his childhood. Then he had gone away to school, and after that had been bear-led all over the continent for a year and they had seen little of him for some time. Then, during Georgeanne's last Season, he had re-appeared and promptly fallen in love with her. He had become quite importunate and "pesky," as Georgeanne put it, "as though he had this prior claim, you know, and it was all settled in some way between us. He has always been so bossy and sure of himself."

Georgeanne had caused not a small sensation at her come-out and at her subsequent appearances in London, and had, to date, received fourteen proposals of marriage and broken countless hearts. As well she might, pronounced Mlle, being as beautiful as an angel and of such a divine good nature. Georgeanne was a silvery blonde with violet blue eyes, a shell-pink complexion, a perfect profile, and dimples, to top off a figure of such perfection that even *one* of the foregoing assets would have caused her to be acclaimed a beauty.

She was possessed also, as Mlle noted, of a sweet, good nature, and was invariably kind to the least prepossessing of her lovesick suitors and even to those of such sour dis-position as Miss Dudham. The only time she ever spoke dis-paragingly of anyone was in the strictest privacy to Dilys. Not even Lady Langthorne was privy to these confidences and often complained that her daughter was too good-hearted and allowed herself to be put upon by the worst bores in London. Georgeanne, however, was in little danger of that, for, despite her kindness to all, she had a knack for achieving her own ends without putting any noses out of joint. Except for Lord Travis. She could not help laughing at his pro-testations of love.

". . . for he is just the same as he was, only taller. He was always so dictatorial, and when I ever dared to disagree with his commands, he would scowl just exactly as he does now. To see him just the same after—what—four years' separation?—somehow only sets me giggling. Of course, that only makes him more furious, but I cannot seem to take him seriously anymore.''

Dilys found this unaccountable, for she knew that if ever he should turn that furious scowl upon her, she would simply shrivel up and die. There seemed little danger of that, however, for he barely acknowledged her existence anymore. She doubted if he had ever truly looked at her. When they had played together in earlier days, she had been but a baby who irritated him by claiming more of Georgeanne's attention than he liked. Her encounter with him in the drawing room when he had been calling Georgeanne a flirt had been her first meeting with him since his return, and he had acknowledged her presence with a distracted nod and returned to glaring at Georgeanne. Of course, she was but a distant cousin and in his eyes but a child, Dilys told herself consolingly. Nevertheless her interest in him continued unabated.

She garnered every smallest item of information about him to record in her diary, and she was privy to a great deal more than anyone quite realized. She was an unusually quiet and unobtrusive little girl who very often went unnoticed when adults were holding conversations not meant for young ears. On occasion her presence was realized and she was invited to run off and play, which bidding she followed without demur. She never sneaked about or hid herself or listened at keyholes, but she felt easy in her conscience about listening openly.

In this way she learned that Lady Langthorne was not at all pleased that Georgeanne had refused to consider Lord Travis as a suitor, for though he was only the younger son of the Duke of Trevithick, he had a grand fortune from his mother and another from a childless brother of his mother's. All this besides the best blood and one of the oldest titles in England, not to speak of the close ties of friendship between the families. "Well, Mademoiselle, you will understand. It was more or less settled between his mother and me, we were bosom bows, you see, that he and Georgeanne would make a match of it someday. I must say, I really cannot understand the girl. He is so very handsome and she has known him all of her life. They always played together so prettily as children, and I had quite settled it in my mind . . . But there, one mustn't despair."

"No, indeed, my lady, it is early days. Perhaps she needs only to accustom herself to the idea of him in a new role."

"Yes, perhaps. I wonder if there is anyone else in her eye? I did think she showed a decided partiality for young Brinton. His father is the Earl of Carleigh, you know, and the boy is the heir. I would certainly be unable to find anything to say against such a match, though I had so hoped . . ."

Dilys had remained undetected throughout this interesting conversation and duly recorded it. She also tackled Georgeanne about "young Brinton" at her earliest opportunity, and was almost positive she saw Georgeanne blush before she turned away and said, "Brinton? Good heavens, Dilly, where do you get such information?"

"Yes, but who is he?"

"Brinton? Why he is the eldest son of the Earl—"

"I know all that. I mean, who is he to you!"

"One of my dancing partners, silly Dilly. Now please speak of something more interesting."

"Oh, do you not find him interesting?"

"Well, he is all right in his way, I suppose," said Georgeanne carelessly. Too carelessly, in Dilys' opinion. There was definitely something in Aunt Sophia's observation.

"Well, I, for one, am glad to learn that you have not developed a *tendre* for him," Dilys said disingenuously, "because I think Travis would be a far better match for you."

"Travis? You are all about in your head, child," cried Georgeanne vehemently. "Why, there can be no comparison. Travis, indeed! With his little infatuation. Henry Brinton is a man, while Travis is but a silly boy. He is—" She stopped abruptly, blushing furiously, aware that she had given away more than she had meant to. "Oh, never mind all that nonsense. I am off for a walk. Will you come?" She walked rapidly away to the door.

Dilys scrambled after her and wisely forbore asking any more questions, though her heart ached for poor Travis, whose love was treated so slightingly.

It was about this time that she first began to think about her own appearance. Georgeanne entered her own room one day to find Dilys gazing intently at herself in the glass over Georgeanne's dressing table.

"Well, do you think you will recognize yourself the next time you meet in the street," Georgeanne asked with a laugh.

Dilys continued her study for a moment in silence. "Georgeanne," she said at last, "shall I look like you when I grow up?"

Georgeanne was so startled she could not think of what to say at first. Finally she faltered, "Well—no, darling, I shouldn't think so, you know. You are dark-haired, you see, and I—"

"Yes, you are fair. I see, yes. What shall I look like, do you think? Shall I be an anecdote?"

Georgeanne giggled. "An antidote, you mean. Certainly not. I am sure you will be lovely."

However, she felt a little pang of unhappiness as she spoke, for she was not at all sure, really. Dilys was such a thin, dark little creature, her hair black and thick, but uncompromisingly straight, and she was all knobby knees and elbows now. Still, she had truly lovely gray eyes and might turn out better than she promised. I will find her a husband, Georgeanne vowed silently, when I am married and living in London. She shall never be left on the shelf if I can help it.

2

Travis has mounted a mistress! I wish I knew what that means exactly, but there is no one to tell me, or at least, no one who would, and even if someone would, there is no one I would ask. Alun would only bluster and tell me to speak to my sister. Sister! As if I could ever call Caroline "sister." And she would only purse up her mouth in that disapproving way she does when I dare to address her at all and ask Miss Poore "why this child is not suitably occupied with her lessons instead of badgering her elders with impertinent questions." Imagine the bad fortune to be a penniless spinster lady saddled with the name of Poore!

Anyway, Travis has clearly misbehaved and I should dearly love to know how. I have seen him only once this last six months, and then not to speak to. I was in the carriage being taken to the dentist by Miss Poore and he was just coming out of White's. He looks just the same, only more beautiful than ever! I longed to call out to him, but lost my nerve. What if he had not recognized me? I should have died of embarrassment. But, oh, I did so long to speak to one of my old friends from the past.

This entry was written when Dilys was twelve, and a great many sad and disagreeable things had happened to her in the intervening years. When she was barely nine, Georgeanne had married her Lord Harry Brinton and gone off with him to India. Dilys had wept for days when she first heard of it, but Georgeanne's radiant happiness had finally shown Dilys that to begrudge it required a depth of selfishness she was not equal to. So she had dried her eyes and tried to be glad for her sister's joy. Eventually she had preceded Georgeanne up the aisle in pink muslin with a wreath of daisies in her hair, feeling proud of Georgeanne's beauty, and very grown-up. When the newly wedded couple had sailed three days later, she tried to remember that adult feeling and not cry—at least not until Georgeanne was gone. Then gloom descended upon her days, and tears were part of every bedtime for weeks.

It was during this sad period that Alun called to announce his impending marriage to Caroline Dudham, and the news that his dear bride desired her new sister to attend her up the aisle. Before she could prevent herself, Dilys cried, "Oh, no! No, never!" and, bursting into tears, had run from the room. Lady Langthorne had smoothed down Alun's ruffled feathers and assured him that of course his little sister would be very happy to attend Caroline. It was only that she was in a depressed state at the moment due to losing Georgeanne.

When Alun had gone away, Lady Langthorne sent for Dilys and chided her mildly for her want of conduct and then explained to her how necessary it was for her to perform this small obligation to her brother. Dilys, not being in the habit of recalcitrance, had at last agreed that she must do so.

She was very much against the idea, however, for had not Georgeanne told her Caroline Dudham was a mean girl? How, then, could Dilys rejoice that her brother was marrying so badly? How join in the festivities that her presence surely indicated her approval of?

Lady Langthorne had said she must attend, and she did, but the setting and circumstances could not help but bring back like circumstances only a few weeks previously when she still had her adored Georgeanne with her. Throughout the ceremony she felt a lump in her throat and could not summon up even the pretense of a smile. She caught Caroline's steely glance directed toward her several times, and knew she had not endeared herself to her new sister-in-law. Indeed, during the reception, as she sat huddled behind a clump of potted palms weeping silently into her handkerchief, she heard Caroline and Alun discussing her as they passed.

"Really, Bryn dear, it is insulting to me for everyone to see a member of your own family lumping about with such a lugubrious expression. I am surprised you will allow her to behave so."

"I am sure no one noticed. Besides, what can I do, Caro, my love?"

"Do? Why, tell her to stop it. She is a child. Children must be told what they must do and what they must not do."

They passed out of Dilys' hearing then, but she made a point of staying well out of Caroline's way until her departure for the honeymoon. They were to be gone for six months and Dilys thought that when they returned, she might not have to see them more than once or twice a year, or at least she hoped not.

In the meantime, there were her letters from Georgeanne, which she spent hours reading over and over and more hours answering. She also spent a lot of time writing in her diary. What time she had left from these activities and doing her lessons she devoted to writing stories, all highly romantic and high-flown, with beautiful doomed heroines and darkly handsome, slightly wicked heroes. She would have preferred to write poetry, but found she had no head for it at all. Her efforts seemed childish even to her own eyes.

Then, not three months after her brother and his bride had returned to England, Lord and Lady Langthorne were drowned together while yachting with friends near Cowles.

Dilys went about the house in a daze of grief, wandering restlessly all day from room to room, unable to eat, her sleep broken by nightmares. She grew pale and thinner than ever and could not be comforted by Mlle. Only Georgeanne could have comforted her, but she was on the other side of the world, pregnant and unable to undertake the long journey home.

Still in a state of numbness Dilys found herself and her boxes being bundled into a carriage one day by a weeping Mlle and being driven away to take up residence with Lord and Lady Bryn. In unquestioning misery she allowed herself to be installed in a room, obeying without demur when told to do this, that, and the other by a strange woman who seemed to be a relative of Caroline's. She had been greeted by Caroline upon arrival and been visited in her room by Alun that same evening, but had seen nothing of either of them for the next four days. Then, at midmorning on the fifth day a servant came to say she was wanted in the drawing room at once. She rose and followed the footman mutely down the stairs. He opened the drawing-room door for her and she walked into the room and there, incredibly, was Lord Travis Gallant.

They looked silently at each other while she felt her eyes glassing over with tears. He sat down and held out his arms, and she ran into them with a cry of anguish and sobbed her heart out onto his exquisitely starched and folded neckcloth. He said not a word, but held her close and patted her shoulder. She never knew that a tear or two of his own stole down his cheeks to drop into her hair. When she had subsided at last into sniffs and hiccups, he solemnly handed her his handkerchief.

"Well, child, you have had more troubles than usual for one so young," he said, smoothing back her hair from her face.

"Oh, Travis—how did you . . ."

"I was in Paris when I heard the news about Aunt Sophia and Uncle Will. I came back as soon as I could—er—straighten out my affairs. I missed the funeral. Then I went around this morning to see you and they told me you were living here with your brother. Is everything all right with you—here?"

"I don't know. I suppose. I haven't really noticed. Oh, Travis—"

"There now, there now. Don't start again because I don't have another handkerchief and my neckcloth could not absorb any more liquid."

This brought a watery smile to her face. "Oh, dear, I have made a mess of it. I am sorry."

"Never mind. Has that—that wife of Alun's been unkind to you?"

"I haven't seen her, really, since the first day. Do you know her?"

"We've met," he replied dryly, "and she received me when I arrived."

"Good heavens! Where?" She looked around wildly, half-expecting to see Caroline's disapproving eye bent upon her from somewhere in the room.

"I told her I wanted to see you alone. She got fairly snippy about it, but I prevailed, as you see," he said with a grim little smile.

He spent a further half-hour with her, being warm and kind and not at all the arrogant, dark-browed Travis she had always known and been partly afraid of. He made little jokes and held her hand tightly if tears seemed imminent. At last he pulled her nearer, kissed her cheek, and rose.

"I'd best go now before madam comes back. I should definitely not care for another encounter with her."

"But—but, Travis, will you come again?"

"Well, I'm off back to Paris in the morning. A rather pressing—er—engagement there, you see. Don't know exactly when I'll be back. But if you should want me for anything, you can always send a note to Gallant House and they'll forward it on to me. You'll be all right now, eh?" he added hopefully. After all, he was only nineteen years old and unused to dealing with children.

"Oh, yes, I will be fine," she said sturdily. "Thank you for coming."

He bowed, patted her head, and left her, her chin well up and a valiant smile on her blotched and tearstained face.

It had faded a moment later when Caroline entered the room. "I hope that young man does not mean to make a habit of visiting you. I have never been treated so arrogantly in my own drawing room before."

"He is my cousin—and Alun's. It was very k-kind of him to come to visit me."

"Ah, so you can speak, I see. I was not sure you could. You have only pouted the times I have seen you. Well, go upstairs again now and let Miss Poore wash your face."

"I am old enough to wash my own face. Is Mademoiselle coming soon?"

"Mademoiselle? Certainly not. You have Miss Poore as governess now."

This was a dreadful blow for Dilys, but she refused to allow Caroline to see that it was so. The hurt it caused joined her general pain and feeling of abandonment. It seemed almost natural that she should lose all her friends and be thrust, without any one consulting her own wishes, into the care of strangers. Her despair at the thought of living with Alun and Caroline roused her for the first time in over a week to thoughts outside her sorrow. What on earth had persuaded Alun to accept her?

Well might she wonder, for indeed Alun had not wanted

to do so in the least, but for once, he had dug in his heels when Caroline, who wanted the child even less, had vehemently declared that she would not have her.

"Well, you must, my dear."

"I *must*? What do you mean, sir? I say I will not have the brat. I dislike her intensely and she dislikes me. Just look at the way she behaved at my wedding. Weeping and glowering at me, humiliating me before all my friends."

"Nonsense. She is only a child. If you put your mind to it, you can charm her to you in no time at all."

"I have no desire to do so, thank you very much. How can you treat me so when you know the delicacy of my condition now?"

Even this reminder of her pregnancy failed to move Alun. "She will be no trouble to you. You need hardly even see her if you don't choose. She has that French governess to take care of her. I am sorry to go against your wishes in anything, my heart, but surely you must see I am constrained to have her. How would it look to everyone if her own brother refused to take a child doubly orphaned in her short life? I should be unable to look my friends in the eye if it ever became known. No, my love, there is no help for it. She must come here."

Caroline knew when she was beaten, but she did not give in entirely. "Very well. So be it," she said coldly, "but only the child. There is no need for the Frenchwoman."

"But surely you will not want to be bothered with her yourself ?"

"Certainly not, but why should we pay wages to the Frenchwoman? I have a spinster cousin of some kind that we pass around in the family for things like this. She will be glad to come as a governess for a room and her meals. She's totally penniless."

So the matter was settled to no one's satisfaction and Dilys was installed in a room on the third floor. Miss Poore was in the room next door. She was the epitome of all middle-aged, downtrodden, penniless spinsters: mousy gray hair in a pitifully small bun, a thin underfed frame, and an obsequious manner. She had been left an orphan at twelve and for the past thirty years had earned her keep by toadying to her relatives' needs—as companion, governess, or general dogsbody. She was barely better educated than Dilys and had little more worldly experience. She was a fidgety little woman, forever leaping from her chair to fetch a handkerchief or a fan or to raise or lower a window or reposition a fire screen, all this activity accompanied by an endless and meaningless pattering of words. Dilys found her patience sorely tried by Miss Poore's perpetual presence, but felt so sorry for her that she succeeded, after she learned her story, in smothering her irritability. Actually, after some months together Miss Poore seemed soothed enough by Dilys' quiet ways and uncritical attitude to relax and not twitter so much. Not so when Caroline made a rare appearance in the schoolroom. Miss Poore sprang from her chair gushing effusive speeches about dear Lady Bryn's looks, dress, and condescension in visiting them.

Though they were distantly related, Caroline allowed no familarity from such a lowly one as Miss Poore, so she was never Cousin Caroline, as would usually be the case. As for Dilys, Caroline had insisted that Dilys must call her Sister, and since Dilys could not bring herself to do so, she managed never to call her anything. Whether Caroline noticed this she never said.

Actually, Dilys saw very little of Caroline. She made the occasional appearance in the schoolroom, she was seen on the stairs at times when Miss Poore took Dilys to the park for an outing, and on several occasions when Dilys was summoned to the drawing room to be presented to one of

Caroline's curious friends. It was on such an occasion that she had heard the snippet of gossip about Travis when, curtsies made, curiosity satisfied, she was allowed to fade away into a window seat. Her presence forgotten after a time, the ladies had begun to talk freely.

Dilys saw her brother even less frequently. She was glad of this, for their rare meetings were occasions of embarrassment to both of them. Really, if she had to live here, she would much rather never have to see either of them. She did not like them and felt quite sure they did not like her, so their meeting could not contribute to the happiness of any of them.

Happiness was not something Dilys felt was ever to be her lot again. Unless, that is, Georgeanne and Harry came back to England and she was allowed to live with them. This seemed unlikely to happen for many years. Harry loved India and Georgeanne loved Harry. Her letters were still rapturous, even more so after her dear little Peter was born, followed in the next three years by two little brothers. She missed Dilys dreadfully, she wrote, and so longed for her. It was the only thorn among the roses of her life. Dilys smiled at this. Georgeanne was always given to such clichés in her letters.

Dilys had not seen Travis again, except for the once on the trip to the dentist. Three years had passed since she had cried on his neckcloth and she was now too self-conscious at twelve to thrust herself upon him; so, though he had said she could write to him, she never had. But she still had his handkerchief, now laundered and folded away into the box that held her few prized possessions: a gold ring with a topaz given to her by Georgeanne, and a necklace of seed pearls from Aunt Sofia. Even his absence, however, could not dim her love for him. Her first childish fascination with him had solidified into love after his visit and had grown steadily ever since. It was the greatest comfort of her life.

3

I have started my new novel! It is to be about Travis. Mlle. said I must stop writing those "Gothick horrors," as she calls them, and write only what I know of, and Travis is the only person I know anything of whose life would be interesting. Mine certainly would not, nor Alun and Caroline's, and though Georgeanne's must be, I know nothing of India and could not depict her life there.

Mlle. had begun writing to Dilys soon after her residence with Alun had begun. Dilys always sent her her stories for praise, and Mlle. did not hesitate to subject them to harsh criticism regarding grammer, punctuation, syntax, and, finally, content.

"You have succeeded in developing an agreeable style," she wrote in her latest, "but it is very difficult to sympathize, or even to believe in, your heroines and their difficulties. What, after all, can a sixteen-year-old girl know of castles in Romania and the possible dishonoring of beautiful princesses? Please forget these Gothick horrors and write of what you can see and know of yourself."

Dilys was quite stunned by this. She had outlined in her head an entirely new and captivating novel about an Egyptian slave girl who was really a Byzantine princess, and she was eager to start it—and why, suddenly, had Mlle. made such a comment? Of course a sixteen-year-old girl couldn't know of her own experience about Romania and all of that, but not many people of any age did. It had not stopped Mrs. Radcliffe from writing *The Mysteries of Udolpho*, had it? And surely Mrs. Radcliffe had never seen or experienced any of those things herself. That was what we were given imaginations for, wasn't it?

Thus kicking, figuratively, against the hard knock her creativity had received, she went about aggrieved and sulky for several days. It was, strangely enough, Miss Poore who brought her to see the matter sensibly. Miss Poore, of course, knew all about the novels. How could she not, when she spent nearly every waking hour in Dilys' company? Besides, over the years they had developed a sympathy for each other to the point where Dilys even allowed Miss Poore to read her novels. Miss Poore thought they were wonderful, quite as good as Mrs. Radcliffe's, she declared.

She was well aware that Dilys' latest had been posted off to Mlle. and that Dilys had been eagerly awaiting a response. She was also aware, when the response was at last received, that it had made Dilys unhappy. At last she gently inquired what was the matter—had Mlle. not cared for the latest romance?

"Oh, it is not that—at least she did not say whether or not on that. She simply says I must try to write about things with which I am familiar."

"Well, my dear, I am sure she is a very intelligent woman and would know best. To me your novels are so very entertaining that I would not know how to fault them. Thankfully, that is not required of me," she added humbly. "But I do think, Dilys dear, if one *is* placed in that position, as you have placed Mademoiselle, and one *does* give a critique, then it behooves you to listen. After all, what is the good of asking someone to read and advise you on your writing if you are unwilling to follow their advice?"

Dilys was much too sensible a girl not to see the soundness of this statement, and her mopes disappeared as she settled down to think about the problem. After much deliberation, as detailed in her diary, she had settled on a novel about Travis. There was, after all, a great deal she knew about him, garnered over years of listening to the gossip in Caroline's drawing room. Travis was by now an accredited rakehell, and his many titivating exploits were retailed with relish by the young matrons pretending horror or disgust: his return to England with a French harlot, his gambling, his duels, his mounting of two, even three mistresses at a time, his flaunting of them by his side at the opera, and on and on. Each week he seemed to commit another outrage. He was no longer received in the best drawing rooms, though Dilys doubted this discomposed him in any way.

She knew, perhaps the only person in London who did, what drove him to such excesses. Her novel, in fact, began, when she finally sat down to write it, with his rejection by a beautiful cousin with whom he had been in love since childhood. Ridden as he was by the devils of despair, he set out to experience every excess possible to help him forget. He is finally redeemed by the love a pure young girl who has been silently devoted to him for many years.

Though she changed his name, and all names of the characters, she limned him truly as boy, as very young man, as he was now, and as she thought he would be in eight or ten years from now when he is finally rescued from hell by the pure young girl.

Once started, the book seemed to almost write itself, the words pouring out of her in a spate as she wrote furiously to keep up with it. Sometimes Miss Poore would have to shake her by the shoulder to get her to stop in time to dress for dinner. For now she was required on most days to take her dinner downstairs when Alun and Caroline were dining

alone, or when her presence was needed at a dinner party
to even the numbers. She would have preferred dining alone
with Miss Poore, but she particularly hated dining in
company, since Caroline invariably put her with some spotty
sprig of the gentry who blushed when she spoke to him and
had no conversation of his own, or partnered her with some
doddering old man who pinched whatever part of her
anatomy was available to him and leered at her revoltingly
while catechizing her on her beaux and how many hearts she
had broken.

If she complained of this degrading treatment, Caroline
only sighed in a martyred way and said she asked so little
of people and would never understand why they must always
be complaining and disagreeable over the least little thing.

"I am sorry to disagree," Dilys said, "but I do not think
being pinched black and blue is the least little thing."

"You always exaggerate everything so dreadfully," sighed
Caroline, rolling her eyes.

"Perhaps you will arrange to have Lord Briars seated next
to you when he comes to dinner again and you will see
whether I exaggerate," retorted Dilys.

"Now you are being impertinent, miss. You may go to
your room."

"Yes, ma'am," Dilys said promptly, and sped gratefully
away.

Caroline had grown quite stout after the birth of her four
boys, all still in the nursery. Though she longed for a
daughter, she had never learned to turn to Dilys for a
substitute relationship. She had determined from the first that
she would not like Dilys, and she had never changed her
opinion. Caroline was not given to changing her opinion
unless it suited her to do so at the time. Dilys had once
overheard her confiding to a friend that Dilys was a constant

source of worry to herself and her husband, being a capricious and sickly child in need of much patience and nursing. To another friend Dilys was described as a quiet little thing, always sitting in corners reading and never opening her mouth in company until really one didn't know how the child would ever be able to conduct herself when she was old enough to go about.

Dilys admitted all this last was, for the most part, true, but Caroline forgot that if Dilys did get into conversation with one of the guests, she was reproved when they were alone for boring people with her foolishness and for trying to draw attention to herself. So Dilys did tend to melt into the farther corners of the room and sit quietly. In this way she learned much that one of such young and tender years should not have heard.

She turned every scrap of gossip into fodder for her book, not all of it about Travis, but of notables of the day in the London *ton*. Sometimes, under protest, she was dragged out by Miss Poore for a walk in the park. "For you will ruin your health, dear child, if you continue in this obsessive way." It was on one of these walks one day that she came face to face with Travis for the first time in five years. She halted in his path, paralyzed by shock and confusion, the color beating up into her face uncomfortably. She stared at him mutely for at least five seconds before tearing her eyes from his face to look at the extraordinary young woman clinging to his arm possessively with both hands.

She was like no other young woman Dilys had ever seen. Everything about her seemed to flash and glitter: her large black eyes, her teeth, earrings, brooches, bracelets, shining black hair, everything. She was ravishingly beautiful.

Travis faltered only a moment before he lifted his hat and bowed slightly. He then led the girl away before Dilys could speak. Dilys heard the girl asking in French who in the world was that solemn little girl, so *arrière-pensée*. Dilys could not hear Travis' answer.

She continued to stand there, unable to believe Travis could be so cold even though so many years had passed since they had last met. There could be no doubt he had recognized her, so why had he not spoken? She felt tears sting her eyes and roll down her cheeks.

"My dearest child, what is it?" Miss Poore asked.

"He did not even speak to me!"

"But who was he?"

"Travis—my cousin Travis Gallant."

"Ah. Well, yes, I see. But really, he behaved quite properly, my dear. He conducted himself just as a gentleman must in such situations."

"But—but—"

"If he had stopped and spoken, he would have had to introduce his friend. And, really, she is not the sort of woman one introduces to one's female relatives."

"Why? What sort of woman is she?"

"Not a—ah—good woman."

"But how can you possibly know that she is not good? She is very beautiful."

"She paints," Miss Poore said succinctly.

"She paints? You mean she is an artist?"

"No, Dilys, for goodness' sakes. She paints her face!" This last was whispered as though it was too horrifying a statement to make aloud.

"Oh. *Oh!* You mean she is his—"

"That will do, Dilys. Come along now."

Dilys forgot her unhappiness. In her head she was rapidly revising the description in her book of Travis' latest mistress. All the way home she recited to herself a list of the girl's attire. No detail was too small to omit. After that, she wanted to walk in the park every day on the chance that she might encounter them again. She never did.

4

Mlle writes that there is a publisher who wants to bring out my book. This is so astonishing that I still cannot quite believe it to be true. Never, even in my wildest daydreams, did it occur to me that such an event could come about—or at least not for years and years and only if I worked very perseveringly to perfect myself. And there is no one I can tell about it, for Mlle says it must never become known that I wrote the book, because it would not be proper for a young girl to become notorious for such a thing, apart from the fact that there are recognizable people in it even though their names *are* changed. I guess I did model some of the characters after people I know, and then there is Travis, of course. But he would never read such a book in any case, so he will never know. Anyway, it is to be published under another name. D. Williams (Mama's family name). I quite like it. Mlle is to deal with the publishers and I am to have fifty pounds. I cannot imagine how she came to send the manuscript to a publisher in the first place. Her criticism was so sharp I quite thought she did not like it at all.

Dilys could not know how very accidentally this had come about. Mlle was now governess to the three lively daughters of the Hon. Mrs. Richard Threese. The eldest of these daughters was fourteen and had read all of Dilys' books on the sly when Mlle went out on her day off. None of the others had been so enthralling to her as this one, however. She became so engrossed that she failed to respond when her mother sent a maid to summon her downstairs. Presently Mrs. Threese went to seek her out and found her curled up on the window seat in her room, rapt with the pages of a manuscript.

"Well, my dear?" Mrs. Threese said good-naturedly.

"Wha . . . Oh, Mama," said the girl, dragging her eyes reluctantly from the page.

"I sent Bessie up for you some time ago," said Mrs. Threese. "When you did not attend me as I requested, I feared something might be wrong."

"Bessie? Good heavens, I do not remember speaking to Bessie. I beg your pardon, Mama."

"What are you so engrossed in, my dear?"

"Oh, Mama, *such* a good story! It is about Lord Travis Gallant, the rakehell."

"And what do you know of rakehells, or of Lord Travis Gallant, if it comes to that?

"Good Lord, Mama, *everyone* knows of him. One cannot help overhearing the gossip."

"Good heavens," said Mrs. Threese, picking up a page and beginning to read it. Then she picked up the next and then the next. She absently sat down in the other corner of the window seat, found the beginning, and started to read. An hour went by before she spoke and then it was only to murmur, "This is not a suitable book for a young girl to be reading." Miss Threese did not reply. She was very near the end now and felt no threat in her mother's tone.

It was some time later when Mrs. Threese's abigail knocked and entered in a most agitated state. "Oh, madam, there you are. I have looked everywhere!"

"Well, you have found me," Mrs. Threese said more sharply than was her usual wont when speaking to her servants. "What is it?"

"Why, madam, it is but a half-hour until dinner, and you not dressed," replied the abigail reproachfully.

"Oh, bother! Very well, go along and lay out my blue. I will be there in a moment." When the maid disappeared, Mrs. Threese turned back to her daughter. "Now, my dear, where did you get this story?"

"One moment," cried her daughter imploringly. She read for less than a moment, then sighed happily. "Oh, it too affecting for anything. The young girl does—"

"Stop," Mrs. Threese commanded. "I do not like to hear the endings while I am still in the middle of a story. Now, I shall ask you again, how did you come by it?"

"I—well, it was sent to Mademoiselle," equivocated young Miss Threese guiltily.

"*She* gave it to you to read?" Mrs. Threese was disbelieving.

"No—not actually gave. She gets these stories from an old pupil and leaves them on her desk in the schoolroom and—and when she goes for her day off, I read them. I am sure she does not mind and I always put them back most carefully," said Miss Threese in an artfully placating manner.

"This is an extremely shocking confession. I find it hard to believe that a daughter of mine could be so underhanded. Do you also read her letters?"

"Oh, Mama, never, never! How could you think so of me?"

"Reading anything of hers without her permission is just as bad. You are to confess to her the moment she returns."

"But you have been reading it also," Miss Threese replied, stung to retort despite the tears of shame rolling down her cheeks.

"That is a specious argument when you know quite well that I was unaware it was Mademoiselle's property. I shall make my own apologies to her, you may be sure. I must now go and dress. Remember, you are to speak to Mademoiselle the moment she comes in, and beg her forgiveness.''

Mrs. Threese swept out of the room on the full tide of her indignation, but made sure to direct her butler to request Mlle to attend her in her dressing room immediately after breakfast the next morning. Mrs. Threese wanted to make her apologies, but she also must, somehow, obtain Mlle. permission to read the rest of that manuscript.

Mlle heard Miss Threese's confession in silence that same evening, read her a stern lecture on the wickedness of her behavior, and as punishment set her a task for the following morning of the declension of some of the more difficult French verbs.

On the next morning, while Miss Threese set to work, Mlle. went to attend upon Mrs. Threese, whose apologies were accepted more graciously, as they must be from one's employer.

"I should like, Mademoiselle, if you will not mind it, to be allowed to read the rest of the manuscript," Mrs. Threese requested humbly.

Permission was given and Mlle. went away to fetch the manuscript and deliver it up to Mrs. Threese, who, needless to say, spent the rest of the morning in her boudoir finishing it, having left word with her butler that she was not in to morning callers. That same night, in the intimacy of the connubial chamber, she told her husband about it and he became interested enough to request a look at it. He bore it away to his dressing room after a final good-night kiss, where he sat up for some hours reading.

The following morning, after he had breakfasted, he returned the book to his wife, who was having her morning chocolate in bed, as was her custom.

"Well, my love, what did you think? Is it not fascinating? Did you finish it?"

"Yes, it is quite interesting, and no, I did not finish it. Just read up to the part where the young girl comes in to save him from himself. Up till then, it was jolly good. Got old Ottway down to perfection, I'd say."

"And those ridiculous Harrison girls and Lady Bellnord with all her pretensions to culture," replied Mrs. Threese with a giggle. "But the most fascinating thing is who could know Lord Travis Gallant so well?"

"Probably one of his bits of muslin out for revenge."

"Oh, Richard, no! No, indeed. It was written by a former pupil of Mademoiselle's. Can you imagine any pupil of hers becoming anyone's bit of muslin?"

"By heaven, you're right there. A great stickler for the proprieties, that woman. Well, well, all very interesting, I'm sure, but I must be off. Good day, my dear."

"Remember, we are to dine with the Coventons tonight," she called after his departing back. He only groaned in response as he disappeared.

Several days later he encountered Mr. Conklin in his club and they stood talking together of a bit of horseflesh Mr. Threese had just purchased, and exchanged views on what each required in an animal before buying. When this conversation had run its course, they stood for some time in a not-too-uncomfortable silence, puffing their cigars and waiting for one of them to think of another topic. After a few moments old Lord Ottway went tottering by and nodded to them, and Mr. Threese remembered the story he had read. And by heaven, here was just the person to tell about it, for Mr. Conklin was half of Conklin, Burrows, Publishers.

"Here's something in your line, Conklin. Read part of an unpublished manuscript some days ago. Not a bit bad, either. Little soppy at the end, but I suppose novels are all like that. Women must have a happy ending, eh? Rarely read novels, myself."

"Yes. They do, yes. Ah, so you liked it, apart from that, you say?"

"Yes, indeed. Walloping good story. About this rakehell, you see. The wife says it's that scoundrel Gallant."

"You mean Lord Travis Gallant? Good Lord. Not by his name, surely?"

"No, no. Names all changed, but recognizable just the same. Lots of others in it I recognized. Old Ottway, as a matter of fact, which is what caused me to remember it. When he passed by just a moment ago, I mean."

"How did you come by this manuscript, if you don't mind my asking?"

"Well, my wife found my daughter reading it, and she started it and liked it so well she put me onto it. Actually, it was sent to my daughter's governess by a former pupil, and my daughter read it while the governess was out, sly little minx," he added dotingly.

"Very interesting. I might take a look at it one day," said Mr. Conklin, and the matter was dropped and by Mr. Threese forgotten. Not by Mr. Conklin, however. He mulled the matter over for some days. Probably only some silly young woman's story, interesting to other young women because it was about that forbidden and forbidding topic, the rakehell. Still, both Mr. and Mrs. Threese had seemingly enjoyed it as well. Thus mused Mr. Conklin.

He let a week go by before mentioning the matter to Mr. Threese again at their club. "Who did you say wrote that story you mentioned to me?"

"Story?" Mr. Threese looked at him blankly.

"That manuscript you spoke of about Gallant."

"Gallant? *Oh*, that. Well, I don't really know. You see, the governess refused to tell us that. She's something starchy, don't you know. A former pupil, was all she would say."

"Ah. I see. Well, shall we order a bite of nuncheon? They do a good bit of beef here, as you know."

Over their beef steaks Mr. Conklin mentioned very casually that he might like to have a look at the manuscript and would it be all right for him to call around some morning. Mr. Threese heartily invited him to come just when he liked.

He neglected to mention this invitation to his wife, so it was with some surprise that she heard him announced one morning. Though friends for years with the Conklins, it was not his habit to pay morning calls upon her. However, she greeted him graciously, ordered wine and biscuits for him, and saw him comfortably seated. She inquired after Mrs. Conklin's health and that of his children, and upon being assured that they were all well, she folded her hands and waited quietly for him to inform her as to the reason for his call.

After some hesitant beginnings, he at last came to the point. Her husband, he explained, had mentioned an interesting manuscript and he wondered if it might be possible for him to speak to the governess in whose possession it reposed.

Mrs. Threese raised a surprised eyebrow, but rose at once and rang for the butler, requesting him to ask Mlle. to step down to the drawing room if it was convenient. Mlle. naturally found it so, and in a few moments was with them. Mrs. Threese introduced her to Mr. Conklin and invited Mlle. to be seated.

"Now—ah—Mademoiselle Fleury, I have been told of a manuscript in your possession that I might be willing to take a look at," he began somewhat pompously.

"For what purpose, sir?" asked Mlle. bluntly.

"Why, I am a publisher of books, madam—er—I beg your pardon—Mademoiselle," he spluttered.

"You wish to publish this manuscript?"

"I must read it first, of course. I could not take it sight

unseen. No publisher would. You could not reasonably expect such a thing.''

''I do not expect it, Mr. Conklin. In fact, I would not dream of the manuscript being published at all. It would be most improper.''

''Oh, Mademoiselle, do not say so,'' Mrs. Threese cried impetuously. ''Why, she might be another Miss Austen. Just think!''

''I very seriously doubt it,'' replied Mlle dryly.

''Perhaps not another Miss Austen,'' Mr. Conklin said, hastily retrieving the conversation before Mlle could become too adamant and unable to change her mind without losing face, ''but nevertheless a contribution to literature.''

''Hardly even that, in my opinion,'' replied Mlle decidedly.

''Still, the author might feel differently about the matter,'' said Mr. Conklin cannily, and knew he had thrown a trump card when he saw indecision replace certitude in Mlle.'s eye. ''Perhaps you would like to consult with her before making up your mind.''

There was further hesitation discernible on Mlle.'s face as she thought this over. She knew very well what would be Dilys' answer, should she be asked—how she would be thrilled to think anyone besides Mlle. would be interested in her writing. Any author would be. Then the expectations aroused and the nervous waiting period, with perhaps, at the end of it all, a negative response from Mr. Conklin and all hopes dashed. No, no, that was not to be thought of. Apart from all this, there was the impropriety of it all. For a pupil of hers to have written such a book in the first place was still a matter of displeasure to Mlle. Not that there was any-thing—explicit—written, but much was implied that a young girl in her charge should not know of. Of course, she had not been in her charge since she was nine years old, and only the good God could know what she had heard or observed while living with the so heartless and cold Lady Bryn.

All of these thoughts were given plenty of time in Mlle's mind, for she was not one to act impulsively. To Mrs. Threese and Mr. Conklin it seemed that centuries of silence were passing, which neither of them dared to break.

At last Mlle. looked up. "I will allow you to read the manuscript, Mr. Conklin, but I commit to nothing beyond that."

Mr. Conklin very quietly let out the pent-up breath he had been holding. "Naturally not, Mademoiselle Fleury. Nor do I."

He carried the manuscript away and spent the rest of the day and the evening reading it. He knew when he finished that he had in his hands a book that would sell very well to the London *ton*, who adored a *roman à clef*. He himself had been fascinated by being able to recognize several characters in it, and though he was not personally acquainted with Lord Travis Gallant, he was very familiar with his scandalous doings, for they had been the talk of the town for several years now, and the writer clearly knew him very well.

After a week he felt he had allowed the pot to simmer long enough, and called once more upon Mrs. Threese. Mlle. was summoned. Mr. Conklin said very blandly that after a great deal of thought he had come to the conclusion that he could probably sell enough copies of the book to justify his publishing it and offered thirty pounds for it. Mlle. stared at him calmly while she made up her mind. She was a shrewd-enough Frenchwoman to recognize a bluff when she saw it.

"Fifty," she replied succinctly, meaning only to test his seriousness, not concede anything.

Mrs. Threese gasped in dismay, but Mr. Conklin replied

instantly, "Done," causing Mlle. to regret that she had not asked for a great deal more. Not that she thought it was worth it, but she would have enjoyed the bargaining.

"And royalties," she said without a flicker of an eyelid to reveal her feeling that she had somehow been tricked into a consent that she had not meant to give.

The matter of royalties being duly settled, Mr. Conklin inquired the authoress's name. Mlle. refused to reveal it, saying that all negotiations would be done through her and the book would be published under another name. Contracts were produced by Mr. Conklin and duly signed by Mlle. in the authoress's name. Mr. Conklin went away an entirely satisfied man.

5

Georgeanne is coming home! In two weeks she will be here. Oh, I am really over the moon with happiness. Now everything will be all right again. It is like life returning to a dead limb. I realize now that I have been only existing all these years, not really living. I have always been waiting for Georgeanne. She is all I have left to love in the world, and the only person who is left to love me. How shall these two weeks ever pass?

I received the money for my book from Mademoiselle and sent half of it back to her, which she promptly returned. But I sent it again with a very firm note, and received in return a stiff, formal little letter thanking me. Dear Mademoiselle, she does so hate sentimentality. I gave Miss Poore ten pounds. I had to be very firm with her also, but at last she gave in. I think it is the first money she has ever had all her own in her entire life!

Alun and Caroline had also received a letter from Georgeanne begging in the most sweetly persuasive way that Dilys be allowed to make her home with herself and Harry so long as she and Harry remained in London. With Miss Poore, naturally.

Caroline was at first inclined to refuse, for no other reason than to be disobliging, but the offer regarding Miss Poore appealed to her stinginess. She could not resist the consideration of how much she would save in food costs with two less mouths to feed. There was no reason at all for this to carry any weight with her, for she and Alun were quite wealthy, but Caroline had miserly instincts, which had grown more decided with the years.

The two weeks crept by and were finally accounted for, and the day came when Dilys and Miss Poore were driven to Harry's town house in the early morning.

Miss Poore went straight to her room, refusing to be present when the family were reunited. "They'll not want a stranger there who must be taken notice of at such a moment, dear Dilys," she had pronounced, and adamantly refused to allow herself to be persuaded otherwise. So Dilys wandered restlessly from room to room, unable to sit quietly or occupy herself in any way. As the hour drew near when they could be expected, her heart began to beat in a queer, not entirely pleasant way.

At last she heard a carriage draw up and rushed to the drawing-room window. Yes, it must be! She ran out into the hall and flung open the outer door just ahead of the advancing butler, who had also been on the alert for the sound of a carriage stopping.

Dilys stopped at the top of the steps, her heart battering away inside her until she could barely breathe, overcome by something she could not have named. It was a compound of shyness and fear that it would not be the same. Georgeanne had her beloved Harry and her three little boys. She could not be expected to feel the same about a sister she had not seen for eight years. Dilys watched as the footman leapt down to open the carriage door and let down the steps. Harry emerged and turned to hand down his wife, and there was Georgeanne! She looked up eagerly.

"Dilys! Dilys," she cried, opening her arms and running forward.

Dilys was down the steps like a shot, and was caught up

in the soft, scented warmness of Georgeanne's arms. Then there were kisses and tears and more embraces. When Georgeanne at last held her off to look at her, Dilys became aware that a large lady in gray holding a baby and three little boys like stairsteps had joined Harry on the pavement, and all, in their various ways, were vastly interested in the scene before them. Harry with amusement, the little boys with wide-eyed wonder, the nurse with impatience at being kept standing about on the damp stones, exposing her charges to the possibility of taking a chill.

Dilys turned from Georgeanne in some embarrassment to hold out her hand to Harry, but he only laughed and gathered her up in a huge bear hug and kissed her resoundingly on the cheek.

"Now, Dilys, here are our young men, all agog to meet their Aunt Dilys," Georgeanne said. "Peter, who is seven, William who is five—"

"Five and a half, Mama," William protested.

"Of course, how very stupid of me, darling. It is all the excitement. William is five and a half, Dilys, and this is Johnny, who is"—she hesitated, anxious not to hurt any more feelings—"three and three-quarters," she finished with a triumphant note.

John beamed at her and in an excess of good will said, before his elder brothers could speak, "How do you do, Aunt Dilys? You may kiss me."

Dilys, who had been longing to snatch all of them and cover them with kisses but was too shy, bent humbly to kiss the warm, round, pink cheek offered to her. Then the two others, not to be outdone in politeness, granted the same privilege.

"And this is our little sister," Peter said, "she is asleep. She sleeps a lot. She was born on the ship and has no country."

"What nonsense, Peter. It was a British ship, so England is as much her country as it is ours," said Georgeanne. She pulled away a corner of the fluffy blanket that shielded the baby's face to disclose the minute mouth just opening in a prodigious yawn, and as Dilys stared, enchanted, the little eyes opened and gazed up mistily at her. Her eyes were the same deep violet-blue as Georgeanne's.

"Oh, Georgie," breathed Dilys softly, "might I hold her?"

"When we are inside, Miss Bryn, and you are seated," the nurse answered authoritatively before Georgeanne could speak.

A slight drawing together of her delicate eyebrows and a deepening of the violet in her eyes were Georgeanne's only expression of her grave displeasure. "Nonsense, Nanny," she said, and taking the baby from Nanny's arms, she put her into Dilys'. "Now, come along, everyone. Into the house. Quickly, boys, up you go." She hustled them all up the steps and into the house, trailed by Nanny, red-faced with indignation, and Georgeanne's abigail, Georgeanne's jewel box in one hand, the other over her mouth to hide her grin at Nanny's comeuppance.

The boys at once shed their outer garments and ran off whooping with excitement to inspect the house. Harry was met by his steward and went away to his own study for a conference. Nanny gathered up the scattered coats and hats and stood grimly in the door of the drawing room, waiting for her precious charge to be restored to her.

Dilys carefully sat down upon a sofa, her eyes riveted to the baby's face. "She looks just like you, Georgie. She is destined to be a great beauty. What have you named her?"

"Dilys Margaret, but because I talked of you so much, the boys became confused and have taken to calling her

Daisy. Of course, she isn't christened yet. I hope you will agree to stand as her godmother?''

"Oh, Georgie, truly? You have given her my name and I'm to be her godmother?''

"Truly, silly Dilly,'' Georgeanne said softly, leaning forward to kiss Dilys' cheek.

"Thank you,'' Dilys said, too overcome to say more, but her eyes blazed with happiness.

Georgeanne stared at her. Why, the child has grown beautiful, she thought. Not pretty. Looking at her critically now for the first time, she saw that it was the eyes that made her beautiful. At first glance one did not realize it. At sixteen she was still slim, but no longer skinny. She was as tall as Georgeanne herself, with a lovely gracefully rounded neck to support her neat, small head. The thick black hair was pulled sleekly back from her face and fell straight and shining down her back. Her face was a pure oval with a fine white complexion, faintly tinged with pink on the cheeks, her nose straight and neat, her mouth still childishly soft and pink, her teeth perfect. And out of this shone the brilliant eyes, large and dark gray, with a darker rim about the iris, set in whites of almost startling clarity. Thick black lashes and eyebrows set the eyes off perfectly.

Impulsively Georgeanne hugged her close, the baby between emitting a soft little squeak of protest. Dilys looked up at that moment and saw the agonized expression in Nanny's eyes. "Oh, take care Georgie! The darling Daisy,'' she cried. She rose and crossed the room to hand the baby back to Nanny. "Thank you, Nanny, for allowing me to hold her. I hope you will not mind if I do so for a bit every day?'' She said this with such a pretty, coaxing smile that Nanny relented enough to mutter acquiescence, before bustling away importantly. Her triumph would have been more complete if that snip of an abigail had been there to see it.

The girls embraced again, then cried a bit from happiness and the sadness they shared, then both began talking at once, with questions and answers and explanations flowing and leaping between them like a stream in spate and somehow neither missing anything, whether spoken or implied by reticence of tone.

The little boys came roaring back into the room and rushed about for a bit before ending in a rolling, struggling heap on the carpet, punching one another and giggling. Dilys was afraid they might do one another an injury, but Georgeanne ignored them and went on talking above the uproar until Nanny reappeared in the doorway. One look at her grim expression and the noise ceased, and when she ordered them upstairs to wash, they trailed out after her, completely subdued.

"Come, darling, let us go up also. I have brought you some lovely presents," said Georgeanne.

There was a case set down in the middle of Georgeanne's bedroom. "There you are. I insisted upon bringing it in the carriage so you would not have to wait. Well, come along, open it up, child."

Dilys looked at the case in wonder. "But, Georgie, all of it?"

"Every bit. Here," she said, flinging open the lid, and Dilys advanced slowly and knelt before it. Hesitantly she lifted out a Kashmir shawl in glowing colors, soft as a cloud. Below it were several rolls of silk in mouth-watering shades of pale blue and green and rose. Then came gold and silver bracelets, and soft leather slippers in red and gold. After that was a foot-high elephant carved in ivory with a howdah on its back and a handsome Indian prince seated inside, regal in turban and silver tunic. At the very bottom was a large sandalwood box with at op inlaid with lapis and ivory. Dilys sat surrounded by all this treasure with the box in her lap.

"Oh, Georgie, so many things—too much. I cannot begin to take it all in. This lovely box—it smells so delicious."

"Open it up," commanded Georgeanne.

Dilys did so and inside was another long blue velvet box. Slowly she opened this and there on a bed of blue velvet was a double strand of perfectly matched pearls, each the size of a large pea, glowing like captured moonlight.

Dilys stared at them a long while in silence before turning to Georgeanne speechlessly. "I started collecting those the first month after I arrived in India. As the eldest, I had the Langthorne pearls, but Mama always said she meant you to have some just as good when you came out. So these are really from her."

Dilys rose and went into Georgeanne's arms and wept upon her shoulder for a bit and felt very much better for releasing so much of the pent-up emotion that seemed to be squeezing her heart and choking her.

Then Georgeanne pulled her to the dressing table. "Sit down, love, and let me fasten them. Oh, they *are* lovely. Perfect with your complexion. Remember the day you asked if you would grow up to look like me?"

"I knew better even then, but I hoped you would tell me you had been skinny and dark too when you were eight and that I would suddenly become beautiful like you."

"Me beautiful? No, no, darling, I was merely pretty. Nothing is more ordinary than pretty girls with blue eyes and blond hair in England. At least half the women are so, it seems to me. But you are truly beautiful, and will only grow more so. You are different—striking—and the best part of it is that it doesn't hit one in the face, but gradually unfolds itself. The more one looks, the more one realizes it. It quite makes one feel superior for having the discernment and taste to have discovered it for oneself."

Blushing with pleasure, Dilys said, "Good heavens, Georgie, I am not sure I find that consolatory—it's even something daunting. To feel I must wait while all those 'ones' find me out. Shall I not be always sitting with the chaperons at balls? Men are slow about 'discovering' that sort of thing themselves, are they not?"

"How wise you are for a young lady barely out of the schoolroom," teased Georgeanne.

"I read a very great deal, and in books it always seems to be the obvious beauties who are asked to stand up at balls."

"Good Lord! Why, I must bring you out while I am here."

"While you are here . . . Oh, Georgie, already you are talking of going away again. How long will you be in England?"

"I am not sure. We came to put Peter and William in school, you see. Six months, possibly eight."

"Oh, could I not go back with you? Oh, pray take me with you, Georgie! I do so hate it not being with you."

"We shall see about that when the time comes, but I promise not to leave you to the whims of the unlovely Caroline again. But you must certainly be presented at a Drawing Room and have your come-out very soon. Has Caroline mentioned the matter at all?"

"Not to me. But I heard her moaning to one of her friends whose daughter was having her come-out about the horrible expense of it all and how glad she was not to have daughters, for they would never be able to afford it."

"She would! Of all the mean, selfish people in the world, she is the worst. Just as well I mean to do it myself. Even if I could shame her into it, she would skimp and make herself a laughing-stock. How unhappy you must have been there, my little girl. I am so sorry. If only I had been here . . . But you must have known how in despair I was when Mama and Papa—''

"Oh, Georgie, darling, don't think of it, now we are together again, and you have Harry and those adorable children. Don't you think Johnny has a look of Travis about him? Those dark brows.''

"Good Lord! Travis. How is he? Do you see much of him?''

Dilys giggled. "I have seen him exactly three times in eight years. Only once to speak to. Oh, Georgie he was so kind to me.'' She told of Travis' visit and crying on his neckcloth.

"And then, the other two times?'' demanded Georgeanne.

"Well, the next time was when I was twelve and being taken to the dentist. I only caught a glimpse of him really. And then a few months ago, I met him in the park—with the most beautiful girl on his arm. But he turned away at once without even speaking. I was very hurt, but Miss Poore explained that she was a—a—''

"Bit of muslin?''

"Yes.''

"Oh, how I should have loved to have seen his face!''

"He was absolutely nonplussed, and so was I.''

This sent them into fits of the giggles. "Poor lad,'' said Georgeanne at last, wiping her eyes. "What an unfortunate encounter.''

"It might have been worse. What if it had been Caroline?''

"Oh, he would have enjoyed that, I'm sure. Probably would have introduced the cyprian, knowing Travis. But you, a pure young girl of his own blood. Oh, never! It was really too bad.'' She went off into giggles again.

The phrase "pure young girl'' had reminded Dilys of her great secret. Should she tell Georgeanne about it? Mlle. had said she must tell no one, but surely she could not keep such a secret from her own sister? She would write Mlle. at once for her advice. She would also ask when the book was to come out. It had been three months now, but Dilys had no idea how long the process of putting a book into print would take. Somehow it seemed less important, though, now that she had Georgeanne.

6

Mlle says under no circumstances to tell Georgeanne about the book unless she asks me outright, when, of course, I could not tell a deliberate falsehood. However, she says this is very unlikely to occur, since, first of all, the book won't be out for some weeks yet, and when it does come out, she would have no reason to associate it with me. She says that if I tell Georgeanne, she will be bound to tell Harry, and he might tell a friend, in strictest confidence, of course, who might tell another friend, et cetera. I can see that she is right, so I won't say anything about it to Georgeanne. Somehow I can't feel very interested in the book anymore—and I doubt anyone else will be interested either. The more I think of it, the more I am surprised that anyone should have wanted to publish it in the first place.

Caroline and Alun came to call on Georgeanne a few mornings after the above entry. It was the proper and expected thing for them to do, but they brought with them such a supercilious air of condescension that Dilys felt quite ashamed.

After greetings had been exchanged and all were seated, Caroline said, ''Well, my dear Lady Brinton, I am quite pleasantly surprised to find you have kept your complexion.''

Georgeanne's delicately arched eyebrows rose a fraction. ''Indeed?'' she replied.

"Yes, after all those years in the Indian sun I expected to see you burned quite brown."

A spot of color tinged each silken pink cheek, but Georgeanne only replied mildly, "I spent very little time out in the sun, I assure you, though Harry is quite tanned. He looks very handsome with it, in my opinion."

"I suppose you must be very happy to be back to civilization again after so many years of roughing it," continued Caroline relentlessly.

"It can hardly be called rough when one lived in a marble palace with at least thirty servants," said Georgeanne evenly, but with an edge to her voice that Alun, at least, heard.

"Ah, Caroline, my dear, I believe your ideas of India are somewhat hazy. Perhaps it will be better to allow Lady Brinton to tell us about it at her own leisure. We hope that you and your husband will dine with us soon. Today week, if that is convenient?"

The intervening week was spent by Georgeanne and Dilys in the acquiring of new clothes for both of them. "I declare I never saw such a collection of drab gowns in all my life, not one fit for a girl in your position. What can that woman mean by dressing you so?" Georgeanne said indignantly.

"What is my position, Georgeanne?"

"You are the youngest daughter of Lord and Lady Langthorne," replied Georgeanne haughtily.

Dilys looked so stricken by this seeming rebuke that Georgeanne relented. "Oh, darling, I am sorry. It was only that I was so cross with the dreadful Caroline. Now, put on your bonnet. We must consult Madame Gris today about your presentation gown and your ball gown, and go for final fittings on the things we ordered from my little woman. I only hope the evening gown will be ready in time for the dinner at Caroline's. I should like her to see how to dress a young girl."

"But Georgie, I was not invited. Alun said quite clearly you and Harry. I was sure at the time that Caroline instructed him to be specific in the matter. Not that I minded. Nothing could be more tedious than one of Caroline's dinner parties. Her friends are all quite dreary and her cook is dreadful.''

"Nonsense, child. Of course they meant to include you. Surely they could not expect us to come to a family party without you. I refuse to believe that even Caroline could be so insensitive and rude.''

"You don't know Caroline,'' Dilys replied darkly.

In the event, she was proved correct, for when they were shown into Caroline's drawing room, she sailed up to greet them, but her welcoming smile froze when she saw Dilys hovering behind Georgeanne and Harry. She shook hands distractedly with the couple, but her eyes were on Dilys.

"Well, well—I am quite at a nonplus—I did not expect— Oh, dear, you will excuse me, I hope—I must consult with my butler—the numbers will be uneven now—no one I can call on at so late an hour—Oh, dear, oh, dear, always these annoying little problems for even the simplest affairs . . .'' She rustled off looking martyred.

Georgeanne caught Dilys eye and winked, and Harry pulled her forward between them as they followed Alun into the room. Most of the guests were known to Georgeanne and Harry, though not well. They were part of the *ton*, certainly, but the sort of people who would be the Bryns' friends, and never the Brintons', including old Lord Briars. When they came to him Dilys dropped a curtsy and edged behind Harry.

The dinner table had been hastily rearranged to seat seventeen people, and Caroline was audibly apologetic to everyone she could manage to speak to about this unfortunate unevenness in the numbers, casting baleful glances at Dilys all the while. Dilys decided to shrug it off. After all, though it was only another of Caroline's thunderingly boring dinner parties, this time there was Georgeanne to look at and exchange glances of complicity with.

It was as well she had this consolation, for there being no gentleman to call upon at so short notice, Caroline had, perforce, to have a woman on Dilys' left. This lady, Mrs. Mills-Overton, vouchsafed only the coldest of nods before turning a shoulder quivering visibly with outrage at the insult. Clearly her hostess considered her as the least important guest and therefore the one to be sacrificed to expendiency, fumed the very angry Mrs. Mills-Overton silently; but to so clearly evince her feelings as to Mrs. Mills-Overton's social importance before everyone was beyond anything. She spent the entire evening plotting her revenge. She felt she could not be so crass as to repeat this same insult upon her hostess and finally came up with a plan to ask her as the guest of honor to dinner and then invite only the lowest of her acquaintances: the curate and his old-maid sister, a doctor and his exceedingly low-bred wife, and so forth. That should serve her right and reveal to Lady Bryn how high she stood in Mrs. Mills-Overton's regard.

On Dilys' right was an elderly gentleman who was too profoundly deaf to make the least pretense at conversation. At least it was not Lord Briars, Dilys thought gratefully. He, she noticed, was next to Georgeanne, but he would never dare pinch her.

This was proved wrong some time later when a muffled shriek sounded from that end of the table and Dilys looked up to see Georgeanne turning disbelieving eyes toward Lord Briars. Dilys buried her mouth in her napkin to cover her explosive laughter and tried to disguise it as a cough. The elderly gentleman on her right became aware of some unusual movement on his left and raised his eyes from his plate long enough to edge her water glass nearer to her reach and then resolutely turned back to his dinner, unwilling to commit himself any further than this.

Dilys did not dare look at Georgeanne through the rest of the meal for fear she would be unable to control the giggles that kept her quaking inwardly. She forced herself to recite the nine tables, always her most difficult, silently for discipline.

This did not help her when the ladies left the gentlemen to their wine and retired to the drawing room, for there Georgeanne came straight up to her.

"That lecherous old goat! I shall have a hideous bruise there tomorrow," she fumed, hardly bothering to lower her voice.

Many amused eyebrows were raised around the room by ladies who had had experience as Lord Briars' dinner partner themselves. Dilys let her long-suppressed giggles have their way with her.

Caroline came hurrying up to them. "Really, you behave like a child, Dilys. I always think it a mistake to have children at the dinner table," she whispered angrily.

"Except when it suits your own convenience, I take it," snapped Georgeanne, too angry herself to mind her manners.

"Whatever do you mean?" countered Caroline, bristling.

"Why, Dilys has written to me several times of attending your dinner parties when she was needed to make the numbers even, as well as having on several occasions suffered the same indignity I myself did this evening. How you can bear to entertain that dreadful old man I cannot imagine."

"He is Bryn's very good friend," retorted Caroline huffily.

"All very well for Lord Bryn. I daresay he doesn't have to sit next to him and get pinched!"

Since Caroline could think of no useful reply to this, she turned to the tiny birdlike lady who came fluttering up opportunely at this moment.

"Ah, Lady Phelps, how nice. I so hoped we could have a quiet coze together before the gentlemen came in."

"Yes, yes, how pleasant that will be—oh, indeed, dear Lady Bryn," twittered Lady Phelps, "but first I must congratulate you upon your dear little sister. She has grown up so charmingly."

"My . . . Oh, yes! Well, thank you. Perhaps we could just sit together over—"

"And the gown is so sweet. Just the thing for a girl of her age. I did used to think that you did not dress her quite—well, not so becomingly as this. I do think your taste is better now. I suppose you will be bringing her out soon," continued Lady Phelps, not noticing Caroline's rise in color at this mention of Dilys' gown, which of course had been chosen by Georgeanne.

"Why, as to that—well, perhaps it is a bit early to be thinking of that. She is much too young to—" waffled Caroline, wondering what on earth had possessed her to invite this irritating woman at all, and resolving never to do so again.

"Nonsense," said Georgeanne briskly, "she is sixteen. I was presented at sixteen. I intend to present Dilys myself, Lady Phelps."

"Well, really, Lady Brinton," sputtered Caroline, all her hackles rising at Georgeanne's tone. "As she is Bryn's own dear sister, I think we are entitled to be consulted in this matter. I am sure we would never do less than our duty."

"Oh, I beg your pardon, you are undoubtedly right," said Georgeanne in a deceptively silken voice. "Naturally, though Dilys is also my sister—legally adopted by my parents, you will remember—I would not want to intervene in any plans you may have made. Only tell me what they are and I will fall in with anything.''

Caroline looked about with a hunted expression. ''Actually, you see, since the child is so young, we have not gone so far as to begin making plans as yet.''

''Perhaps you would like to consult with your husband and tell me what you decide. I would defer to your wishes if you feel that your claims of relationship are stronger than my own.''

Caroline's eyes lost their glazed look as she saw her way out of the trap of her own making. ''My dear Lady Brinton, no, indeed! You were two sisters always, and sisters are always closer than they can be with a brother. Naturally, you must have your own way in this, and I know Bryn would agree with me. We would not dream of interfering. Do tell us what you have planned.''

Georgeanne gave a little gurgling laugh, not in relief, for she had never for a moment believed that Caroline truly meant to do anything for Dilys but had only reacted in her usual contrary way. Her laugh was at the ridiculousness of the little scene just played out. She could hardly wait to get home and confide it to Harry.

''Truly, you would not believe what a fool she made of herself, my love,'' she said to Harry. ''I can read her like a book. She rushed in, all outraged, to take the bait and then retreated so pitifully when she saw that she was caught by her own wrongheadedness.''

''I cannot think why you bother with her at all, my love. You should just have announced your intentions and ignored her.''

''Oh, but it so much more amusing this way, and it makes me feel so much cleverer than I am to know how to manage her. You see, if I had not given her the option, she would have gone all about town saying I was behaving high-handedly and that sort of thing.''

"Well, I only hope you were not so amused you will seek them out for entertainment often, for I find them both deadly bores, and their friends worse," grumbled Harry.

"That is because you will not see the fun in it. If you would only—''

"Oh, enough of all that. We surely have better things to do." He pulled her into his arms and proceeded to demonstrate what those things might be.

Caroline was feeling triumphant also. "You will never believe how clever I have been," she cried to her husband when the last guest was gone. "She tried very hard to force me to bring Dilys out, but I turned the table on her very neatly and landed the problem back in her own lap.''

"But it is our duty, perhaps, to do the thing ourselves. I would not have people think—''

"Oh, what nonsense! Do you have any idea what it would cost? The gowns, the ball—why, it would be a monstrous expense.''

"Well, no doubt you are right, but still I would not like people to think me so behindhand with the world I could not afford to pay.''

"Pho, pho, pho, sir. You care too much what people will think. What of me? Can you not think of me? Think of all the work involved in giving such a ball. And then afterward I should have to chaperon her all over town day and night. Can you tell me how I can attend to my own household and mother my little boys with all of that to do as well? Why, I should no doubt fall ill and go into a decline from exhaustion. Is that what you want? Shall I sacrifice my health to these mysterious people you keep on and on about?''

It was quite three-quarters of an hour before poor Lord

Bryn was able to convince his wife that he had meant no harm to her and would never dream of doing anything to endanger her health. They parted for the night at last, both feeling quite satisfied, for Alun was only too happy to be persuaded not to spend his money and Caroline felt herself a master at knowing how to bring people around to fall in with her own wishes.

Dilys began to record the evening's events in her diary, but presently her thoughts turned to the gown she was to wear and she tried to picture herself in it floating about the ballroom in the arms of some faceless young man. Then the face became that of Travis, his dark-browed glower turned down upon her. Her heart began to thump with fear at his imagined displeasure. She blew out her candle and pushed her face into her pillow to drive his image away, but it persisted. Would he even come? Would he dance with her if he did? Oh, but surely he would have to. Georgeanne would make him do so, and he would be cross and glare at both of them, for, of course, he would want to dance with Georgeanne. But he would not come. He never attended such affairs. Probably had already forgotten her existence. But surely he would come, for he was her cousin. But it seemed most unlikely that he would. And if he did, would he . . .

7

Daisy is to be christened next week and I am so excited about it. Nurse has been very kind, really, and lets me hold the baby ever so long. I make a point of always sitting down before I take her, and that makes Nanny happy. Daisy is really the dearest little girl in the world—so soft and smiling all the time. She hardly ever is fretful as some babies are. Caroline's youngest cried continuously, I remember.

My presentation is tomorrow and my gown is so unbelievable, but those wide panniers and train, I feel as though I'm going to a costume party! I only hope I don't bobble when I make my curtsy to her majesty. I am really quite besotted with my gown for my ball. (That sounds so imposing. My ball! My very first and my own, given for me!) Anyway, the gown is white gauze with spangles and the palest blue ribbands—quite plain, really, but so very elegant, just the sort of thing Georgeanne would choose. And her own gown! A bluey-violet that almost exactly matches her eyes— she looks quite divine in it.

The fittings for these gowns and many, many more that had been ordered by Georgeanne for Dilys and for herself took up several hours every day. Other hours were devoted to shopping for the fans, shoes, stockings, gloves, and bonnets to go with the various costumes. There were also hours devoted to making necessary calls upon relatives.

These were mostly Harry's relatives, for she had only two old aunts living in London. Of course, there were also hours that must be given to receiving calls when they were at home.

Shortly after the above entry, Dilys and Georgeanne were entertaining one of the old aunts, Lady Sommers, who was nearly eighty and who had come to inspect Georgeanne's children. The little boys were lined up before her while Daisy reposed in her lap. The baby had just given her a tremulous gummy smile and old Lady Sommers stared down at her bewitched. Then she cleared her throat, said "Humph," and forced her eyes away. She raked a searching glance over the boys. "You may kiss my cheek," she said to them magnanimously.

The boys froze and their eyes slid around to their mother. She smiled encouragingly and gave a small nod. Obediently they stepped forward one at a time and manfully did their duty by planting a kiss on the withered cheek.

"Humph," said Lady Sommers. "Well-brought-up so far. But you must beware of spoiling them, Georgeanne. There is nothing more disgusting than a spoiled child. Only think of Travis! Ravaging around the continent creating scandal and then bringing his light-o'-love back with him. All rouge and feathers. I saw him myself at the opera with her, and he dared to bow to me. From his box, of course. He at least knew better than to approach me in company with such a creature. But there it is, spoiled from the moment he first drew breath. Oh, I warned his mama many a time, but she would never listen to me. No more would his nurse or anyone else in that household. He was such a pretty little fellow, you see, with such winning ways. Sly, I called it. Knew before he could speak just how to work his wiles on the pack of them. Of all the perfect examples of the results of early spoiling he is—"

"Lord Travis Gallant, my lady," announced the butler as he opened the door at this moment.

Travis hurried into the room upon the butler's heels. "Well, Georgeanne, you are back. You might at least have . . ." He stopped abruptly as the battery of six pairs of eyes turned upon him. The little boys stared at him in fascinated awe to have so instantly presented to them, like an illustration in a book, this epitome of spoiled boy. Lady Sommers' eyes flashed with interest, for of course she adored Travis and had spoiled him as badly as anyone when she had the chance. Georgeanne's eyes brimmed with laughter at this delightful development. Dilys' were as wide as the boys, while Daisy had fallen asleep and missed everything.

Georgeanne rang for Nanny, who was only outside in the corridor, and she bustled in to relieve Lady Sommers of her burden and herd the three boys out of the room.

"Well, Travis, how good of you to come around," said Georgeanne with a wide, unabashed grin at the richness of the situation. "Here is your Aunt Sommers. She was just telling us of meeting you at the opera."

Travis turned and trod dutifully across to his aunt to bow over her hand. "Aunt Sommers. I hope you are keeping well?"

"You do, eh? I would never have guessed it from the way you have never come near me for these past six months. I might have been dead and buried for all you knew."

"Oh, surely such dire news would have reached my ears had so unfortunate a thing occurred," he replied.

"Yes, and you would have come running around then to see if I had left you anything in my will, no doubt."

"I think I know better than to have any such unrealistic expectations, Aunt."

"Sauce," she sniffed, and rose. "I will bid you good day,

Georgeanne. Dilys, I hope you are not going to be such a fool as to become all romantic about your coming-out. Keep your wits about you and remember you are there to be seen by eligible young men, and don't fall in love with the first scoundrel with soft words on the lookout for a fortune.''

"Oh, Aunt Sommers, I hope there won't be any scoundrels at my ball," Dilys said.

"They are all scoundrels," pronounced Lady Sommers with a dark look at Travis, and with that she sailed out of the room, followed by Georgeanne to see her to the door.

"Silly, interfering old bag of bones," muttered Travis, his dark brows meeting in a frown of displeasure as he turned away impatiently to pace to the window and stand staring out into the street. Some two or three minutes of silence ensued before he turned abruptly back to the room and gave a start of surprise at seeing Dilys sitting composedly upon the sofa watching him.

"What the devil! Beg your pardon, but you took me by surprise. Who the dev—I mean, who are you?''

"Dilys," she replied simply, not at all disconcerted, for she would have been more surprised if he had remembered her.

"Dilys?"

"Your cousin, Dilys Bryn. I expect you have forgotten me?''

"Well, yes, I suppose I had. Besides, you were only a child—''

"Yes, I was, but I grew up, you see, just as you did.''

"I can see that you have," he replied gravely.

"I believe you also recognized me in the park some months ago," she said.

"In the park?''

"Yes, you were with a young lady and—''

"Oh, yes, I thought you looked familiar. But you still looked a child then.''

"That is because Caroline, my brother's wife . . . Do you remember Alun? Perhaps not, though. In any case, Caroline would not let me put my hair up and she dressed me unsuitably for my age."

A gleam of amusement lit his eyes. "And what age would that be?"

"Sixteen."

"A very great age, indeed."

"You need not talk down to me, Travis. I realize it seems young to one who is six-and-twenty. *That* is a very great age."

He looked stung and had opened his mouth to retort when Georgeanne came back into the room and he forgot Dilys once again.

"Georgeanne," he cried, and hurried forward to take up both her hands and kiss first one, then the other.

She pulled them away gently with a laugh. "Still the same impetuous boy as ever, Travis. Now, sit down, please, and tell me all about your life while I have been away."

"What life? I have no life since you—"

"That is not what I have heard," she teased. "My sources say you have had perhaps too much life."

"Pah! I have passed the time, tried to forget you and—"

"And succeeded very well," she finished for him. "Now, Travis, Dilys will be having her come-out ball in a week. I will send you a card."

"Do not put yourself to the trouble," he said crossly.

"Nonsense, it is no trouble at all. Naturally, as Dilys' cousin you will want to be there."

"Will you stand up with me?"

"Dilys and I will both stand up with you, of course. Will we not, Dilys?"

"Do you dance, Travis?" Dilys asked.

"I detest dancing," he replied grittily.

"Then, no, thank you. I intend to be very gay and I should be quite depressed to be dancing with someone who detests it," she said, though a hope she had nurtured deflated within her. However, she would not let him know she cared one way or the other. Really, he was quite odious, and she wished she did not love him.

"You are right, my love," said Georgeanne, her lips twitching mischievously. "It will pay him out if no one will stand up with him."

"I do not know that I will come, in any case," he replied arrogantly.

"No, I shouldn't if I were you," Georgeanne said agreeably. "No doubt you will be monstrously bored."

"I think he should make an appearance whether he dances or not," said Dilys. "After all, I haven't all that many relatives and they should rally 'round now and—and—protect me from scoundrels and fortune-seekers. Have I a fortune for them to seek, Georgeanne?"

"Well, of course you have. I mean, not one of the great heiresses, perhaps, but enough. Do you tell me Alun has never discussed this matter with you?"

"No, never. I assumed I was penniless as well as orphaned. Caroline was forever hinting at the terrible burden I was, though I never paid any heed to that since she *is* a great heiress and Alun inherited all the Bryn money."

"Really, that woman should be put out of her misery. It would be a kindness," cried Georgeanne indignantly. "The fact is, Dilys, you were left Lady Bryn's money, some fifteen thousand pounds, I believe, and you and I shared equally Mama's and Papa's estate, which is a very tidy amount indeed. You will receive your fortune when you are married or when you are one-and-twenty, whichever comes first. In the meantime, Alun was given five hundred pounds a year for your upkeep all the while you have lived with them."

"Well! Aunt Sommers was right. I shall need protection from scoundrels and fortune-hunters," said Dilys with gratification.

"Yes, that quite settles it. You will have to attend the ball, Travis. You are the very person for the job. I am sure you will be able to point out every scoundrel and fortune-hunter in the room," said Georgeanne gaily.

He scowled. "Were those all your children? The ones who were here when I came in?" he asked abruptly.

"Well, of course they are my children. Whose did you think they might be? Three boys and a girl, and I hope there will be more in time."

"Good God!" He stared at her bleakly for a moment, then turned on his heel and stalked to the door.

"Surely you will wait to see Harry?" called Georgeanne. He kept going. "Travis!" He stopped at that and turned. "It was good of you to call. I hope you will come often to see us." He bowed briefly and turned to the door. "Dilys and I will look forward to seeing you, will we not, Dilys?"

He took the hint and turned, bowed to Dilys, and then went out the door.

"Well, really," exclaimed Dilys indignantly. "He can never seem to remember I am even in the room. He is the most infuriating man I have ever known! And he is still in love with you."

"Oh, that is only a habit he has gotten into. It was never real, you know, only calf love to begin with, and afterwards a convenience to protect him from predatory females. I think the sight of all the children cast a pall over his romantic notions today," said Georgeanne, gurgling with laughter. "Poor Travis, he was never cut out to be the tragic hero."

"Oh, I think he was. So dark and brooding-looking."

"And so rude and arrogant."

"He was very kind to me once," Dilys said wistfully.

Georgeanne, startled by something in her voice, studied her alertly for a few seconds. "Oh, yes," she said lightly, "there is a great deal of good about Travis despite his reputation. He never flirts with young susceptible girls, at least not one who can be accounted a lady; he gambles, but never ruinously; he is good to his servants and they worship him. That is always a good sign. But it is more than time for him to stop all this nonsense and settle down and start his own nursery. He will make a good husband, I think, once he has been taught some manners. I must put my mind to the problem."

Dilys began to feel apprehensive. What did Georgeanne mean to do? Find a wife for him? Naturally, if she seriously meant to put her mind to the problem, she would prevail. Georgeanne always prevailed. Who would she feel suitable for Travis?

Dilys had never considered the possibility of Travis becoming her own, despite her love. He had always seemed as unavailable as the North Star. He had always loved Georgeanne, and despite Georgeanne's disclaimer of "calf love," Dilys felt he, tragically, loved her still. She could only empathize with him, for she felt her love for him was as hopeless as his love for Georgeanne.

However, if Georgeanne was going to find a wife for him and persuade him, somehow, to settle down and start his nursery instead of continuing as a love-doomed rakehell, then Dilys thought he might as well settle down with herself. She would like very much to enlist Georgeanne's help in this, but could not imagine confessing her love, even to Georgeanne.

I must just put my mind to the problem, she thought. After all, the pure young girl in my book accomplished it alone— and it was I who showed her the way!

8

The christening was the most divinely religious experience of my life! Dearest little Daisy never cried at all, but smiled at everyone throughout the whole thing, including her godfather—Travis! Now, would anyone have expected that? I was speechless when Georgeanne told me that she had asked him and that he had accepted. When I told Caroline he was to be Daisy's godfather, she said Georgeanne was as clever as she could stare for choosing a wealthy bachelor who would be sure to leave everything to a goddaughter. I replied that he was a young man still, that no doubt he would marry and have children of his own to leave his money to, but she only laughed in her insinuating way and said a man with his wild tastes was unlikely to tie himself down with a wife. I wanted to box her ear!

Still, even I can hardly believe it really came about, even though we stood there at the font, side by side. At first I was so flustered I could barely concentrate on my duties as godmother. The oddity of it all seems to have caused something of a stir in the *ton*, used for ages to condemning poor Travis as a rakehell and not inviting him to their parties. At least those ladies do not who have no daughters to push. Those who do will invite any man, no matter what his reputation, especially those mamas with unprepossessing daughters who haven't "taken" after being out three or four Seasons. And who can blame them? Poor women—

condemned to shame for not getting a husband, and untrained to do anything else. Maybe I'll write a book about that. The girl will be plain but brilliant—and will become a famous writer rather than marry just for the sake of escaping the shame of spinsterhood. Anyway, we have seen Travis several times at parties recently. No doubt the ladies feel that if he is acceptable to Georgeanne, who can do no wrong, then he must be safe. Though most of them look somewhat edgy when he is announced. He never seems to be enjoying himself, just stands about scowling, mostly at Georgeanne. He never much notices me, beyond a civil greeting.

This entry was written two days before Dily's coming-out ball, and the hours that followed were so filled with preparation they sped by almost too rapidly. In the odd moments between tasks Dilys was subject to terrifically active butterflies in her stomach, a sensation she dreaded, for it made her feel rather queer and sick with dread and anticipation.

All the reception rooms positively glittered with polish, and the ballroom was banked with flowers on the afternoon of "the day" when Dilys and Georgeanne toured the house for a final inspection. There were to be thirty to dinner before the ball, and the maids and footmen were still swarming in and out of the dining room dressing the table with china, silver, and crystal.

Dilys read one of the beautifully hand-lettered menu cards set before each place in silver holders. "Oh, Georgie, it all sounds delicious," she cried, but then her stomach fluttered and she hastily replaced the card. "Though I doubt I shall be able to eat any of it."

"You won't have to, dearest. You can toy with it daintily. No one will notice. Now I think you should go up and have a nice quiet lie-down before it is time to dress for dinner.''

"Oh, I shan't be able to lie down for more than two minutes. I am far too nervous.''

However, she did as she was bid, and when Georgeanne peeked into her room a half-hour later, she found Dilys sound asleep and was told by Miss Poore that Dilys remained asleep until waked by her abigail for her bath. Moreover, when they were finally sitting down to dinner, she noticed that Dilys ate as heartily as any healthy girl could be expected to do, all the while talking away gaily to young Lord Withers, who had brought her in to dinner.

Georgeanne had meant that honor for Travis, but he had brusquely informed her that he was entertaining his friend Burton to dinner that evening. She was annoyed, for she felt sure he was doing no such thing, but she bit her tongue on any antagonizing retort, being intent upon securing him for the ball at least.

"You will, I hope, do Dilys the honor of coming later.''

"If I have the time,'' he said airily.

Georgeanne ground her teeth silently and prayed that his conscience would turn the trick in her favor, for she knew well that whatever Dilys might say to the contrary, she would be hurt if he did not come.

Indeed, Dilys had felt the sting of his refusal to come to dinner, but after some thought she had decided she would not allow her disappointment to spoil the day for her. After all, she could only have one come-out and she wanted it to be something she would remember with joy.

She was sorry that Georgeanne had felt compelled to invite Alun and Caroline to the dinner, but was glad of it when she saw Caroline's outraged glare across the table at Miss Poore, who had never looked so well in her life. Georgeanne had had a gown made for her in dove-gray silk trimmed with creamy lace and pale-lavender ribbands. Her hair had been becomingly dressed by Georgeanne's own abigail and covered with a frothy lace cap. The real difference, however, was her general air of quiet happiness. She had lost most of her fidgety habits since coming to live with Georgeanne and Harry, for they treated her as one of their family and always with kindness and courtesy. Her views were solicited and heeded, and her offers of help in attending to Georgeanne's correspondence, or taking the boys out on various expeditions, were received with honest gratitude. Nanny had become her confidante and she was always welcome in the nursery. Life for her was bliss. She relaxed and ate more and had filled out becomingly and acquired a faint flush of color in her cheeks. She breathed contentment.

When she looked up at the dinner party and saw Caroline glaring at her, she gave her a sweet smile and a gracious nod and turned away to her dinner partner, Sir Wicklow Pryce, a country neighbor of Harry's, who had been invited especially to partner Miss Poore.

"He is an old dear and was your father's close friend. I am sure he will be gratified to be invited and he will treat Miss Poore wonderfully. I do not want her intimidated by all the grand titles," Georgeanne said to Harry, who wrote off to Sir Wicklow and received his delighted acceptance within three days.

Nothing could have been more gallant that his behavior to Miss Poore, and nothing could have soured the evening more for Caroline then seeing her former wretched dogsbody "putting on the airs of a duchess," as she fumed to herself silently. Caroline did not appreciate being forced to sit down to dinner with someone considered little better than a servant, for all that the person was related to her.

For Dilys it was a grand start to her evening, and contemplating the situation caused her to forget her butterflies and eat everything put before her without even noticing it as she tried to draw out shy Lord Withers.

There was another young man at the table who drew her eyes like a magnet, for he was undoubtedly the handsomest man there. He was Lord Cleveland, a friend of Harry's since Oxford, with fair hair, perfect features and a tall slender frame. When the gentleman rejoined the ladies after dinner, Lord Cleveland managed to reach Dilys four steps ahead of Lord Withers, who had been too shy and tongue-tied to bring himself to say much of anything during dinner, but now had resolved to ask her to stand up with him for the first set.

"Miss Bryn, dare I hope you are not yet engaged for the first set?" said Lord Cleveland with all the urbanity of his twenty-eight years over Lord Withers nineteen.

"Oh, but I—" exclaimed Lord Withers.

"Yes, you may dare hope, Lord Cleveland, and yes, I will happily accept the invitation," Dilys said, much gratified.

"Then I must resign myself to being beaten out by legs only an inch or so longer, and request the second," Lord Withers said ruefully.

"My legs may have given me the edge on reaching her first, but you had the advantage of partnering Miss Dilys at dinner and so had your opportunity, young Withers," retorted Lord Cleveland with a grin. He proceeded to request another set for after supper.

By the time the music struck up for the first, Dilys' card was full, and filled with confidence at so gratifying a circumstance, Dilys took Lord Cleveland's arm and sailed out onto the floor with a radiant smile and not a single butterfly. No partner could have been more to the advantage of a young girl opening the ball for the first time than Lord Cleveland. He was all smiles and gallantry, complimenting her lavishly and flirting mildly. He was not in the market

for a bride, even if she was Brinton's sister-in-law, nor was
he in the habit of trying to attach green girls when he had
no serious intentions. He knew to perfection how to make
love lightly while dancing without giving his partner any
untoward ideas.

Since Dilys' heart was already given away, there was no
possibility of her developing a *tendre* for the first handsome
man she stood up with, any more than the second or any
who followed after. That did not mean that she did not enjoy
the flirting, even when it was executed with more serious
aims than Lord Cleveland's, for there were more than a few
young and not-so-young men in attendance who were on the
lookout for a bride with a fortune, and word had not been
slow to spread, and exaggerate, Miss Bryn's prospects.

However, even in the midst of all this gaiety and breathless
excitement, Dilys kept a sharp eye out for Travis, who had
still not made an appearance when she was handed downstairs to supper by a cluster of young men. He did not appear
actually until the second set after supper. He did not even
look around, but went straight across the room to
Georgeanne.

When Dilys was returned to Georgeanne by her partner,
it was clear there had been some disagreement and they were
no longer in charity with each other, for Travis glowered
down at his toes, and Georgeanne's blue eyes had deepened
to a stormy violet. She smiled determinedly up at Dilys and
her partner, however, and began a light conversation with
the young man.

Dilys turned to Travis. "Good evening, Travis. I am very
happy that you could come," she said politely.

His head came up with a jerk and he stared at her blankly.
"I am Dilys. You remember—your cousin," she said kindly,
with only the barest edge of irony discernible in her tone.

"I *know* who you are," he cried irritably.

"And good evening to you too, Dilys," she murmured.

"Sorry. Of course I did not mean to be rude."

"Did you not?" She widened her eyes at him in amazement.

"No, I did not," he snapped, but then he could not help smiling. "What a little brat you are still. I remember you were always used to taking those sly little digs at me."

"Good heavens, that surely cannot be so. You snubbed me so terribly that I hardly dared open my mouth in your presence."

"Nonsense. Now, I trust your ball is being all you hoped?"

"Oh, more. Much more!"

"Yes, I can see you are enjoying it. I hope you will stand up with me for a set."

Now Dilys' amazement was genuine. Much as she had dreamed of dancing with him, she had given up all idea of it for tonight. "I am sorry, but every set is taken. And you did say you detested dancing and I said then that I would not stand up with you in that case, if you remember. Besides, it is very late, Travis. You cannot expect me to have a set left at this hour. I should consider myself a complete failure if I could not fill every set at my own come-out ball by this time."

"Then I will wish you good night," he said, and with an abrupt bow left them. He did not leave altogether, however, for during the next set, which was a waltz with Lord Cleveland, she was surprised to see him lounging against the doorpost, staring at her. At least he seemed to be staring at her, for, as she moved down the room and turned again, his eyes had followed her progress. On the next turn he was gone, and her spirits sagged momentarily. They rose again in a moment as she told herself that he had made an appearance—and he had asked her to stand up with him. More than that, he had, for once, seemed to be aware of her being in the same room with himself. She was very glad that he had seen her while Lord Cleveland was her partner, for he was so handsome and he smiled into her eyes all the while they danced. She smiled back resolutely and put Travis out of her thoughts for the rest of the ball. After tonight she would give him her full concentration.

It was four in the morning before the musicians put away their instruments and nearly an hour after that before Dilys had a chance to speak apart with Georgeanne as they went slowly and wearily up the stairs together.

"What on earth did you say to Travis to make him so cross?"

"Oh, he is so stupid I have no time for him at all anymore," sighed Georgeanne. "I thanked him for coming and he said he had only come to stand up once with you and me and then would leave. Then I said he was rude and he said . . . Oh, I do not remember it all! Only the upshot was that I declared that nothing could be less agreeable to me than standing up with someone who only wanted to quarrel, and then you came up. All foolishness, you see, and typical of Travis."

"Ah, poor fellow, though, Georgie. He did make an appearance for my sake, and then neither of us would stand up with him."

Georgeanne laughed. "Yes, poor boy, though I must admit your little set-down was delightful. It will do him no end of good to discover that not every woman in the world is holding her breath for a kind word from him. No doubt he enjoyed a terrific temper tantrum after he left."

Indeed, Travis' temper had held him in its grip for nearly twenty minutes after he left Brinton House. He strode along muttering to himself things like "little minx!" and "cursed brat!" and "I should have boxed her ear," and slashing with his cane at any lamppost that presented itself.

Then, presently, he began to cool down, and as he rehearsed the scene in the ballroom, his lips began to twitch and then he laughed out loud, causing a gentleman approaching him to start apprehensively and quickly cross the road.

Still, he thought, she is a little brat, standing there telling me why she would not dance with me with all the self-possession of a twenty-year-old beauty with more proposals than she could count. And looking so absurdly young. Well, of course, she is young. She hasn't turned out badly, though, considering. He remembered her as a very plain child tagging after Georgeanne and himself in their games, all eyes and gawky elbows.

Not gawky now, however. He pictured her again spinning down the room in Cleveland's arms. He gnashed his teeth and then laughed at his own absurdity. Why should she not dance with Cleveland, or any of the others? They at least had made a point of coming early enough to secure a dance, while his own pigheadedness had kept him away.

He arrived home in a much better frame of mind and allowed himself to be divested of his clothing by his man and helped into his nightclothes. When the valet retired, Travis threw himself into a chair before his bedroom fire and lit a pipe. As he stared into the flames, he suddenly thought of Georgeanne and realized he had forgotten all about their little quarrel. His anger, he now realized, had been all for Dilys.

He set himself deliberately to ponder upon his feelings for Georgeanne. After a time he was forced to the conclusion that his old, habitual, and time-honored love for her was just that—old, habitual, and time-honored. He had been, all these years, like a child determined to have what had been denied him, still stubbornly kicking his heels and howling on the nursery floor long after the desire for the object had been forgotten. If he was completely honest with himself, he would have to admit that the desire had died long ago—not six months after her marriage, in fact. Since then, he had had many affairs and rarely thought of her for months at a time. Not that he had not been in love with her at the time, for he had been, but he saw now that it had been a boy's infatuation and would never have done. They would have been at each other's throat constantly and eventually love would have turned to loathing. They were too much alike, really, both spoiled and used to having their own way.

Well, well, he sighed, stretching his long legs nearer the fire, perhaps I am not meant for marriage. I have never met anyone since Georgeanne who tempted me into falling in love, much less proposing marriage, and I am certainly getting older. He heard Dilys saying, ". . . six-and-twenty. *That* is a very great age."

What a brat it is, he thought, grinning into the flames. I shall end up boxing her ear for sure one day.

9

It has been ever so long since I have had a moment to write, and so very much has happened that I do not know if I shall ever be able to remember it all and catch up on my diary. And these are the very details one will want to remember someday in the future. In spite of a perfect whirl of activity now, I know it cannot go on forever and then I will want to start on a new book—and I have decided it will be about the plain but brilliant girl who refuses to marry just for the sake of it.

Anyway, every morning we entertain many visitors: Lord Cleveland, Lord Withers, Mr. Ogilvy, Sir Twistleton Crofton, Mr. Burleigh, and Lord Daventry (he is very old and wears stays and is penniless; they say he has been on the lookout for an heiress since his wife died fifteen years ago, and has proposed to hundreds of young ladies). Several bouquets arrive every day and I am in danger of getting quite above myself with all the flattery and flirtation. Or I should do so if I were not convinced it is all for the dowry. I haven't noticed any signs of any of them being really in love, in spite of all the things they say, which I hope I will never be such a fool as to believe, since I know perfectly well that I could never be acclaimed as a great beauty—or even a lesser one. The rest of the day after the callers have gone is filled with racing around from one party to another and incessantly changing one's clothes, and nearly every night another ball or a grand dinner party—sometimes both.

I see Travis more frequently now, though he has not
come to call; he seems to be invited most places. He
never dances, so I suppose it is true that he detests it.
He is always polite when he speaks to me, but he seems
to be glowering at me all the rest of the time. Perhaps
he is afraid I will disgrace him in some way.

This entry was written in the very early morning some days
after Dilys' own ball, and it was on this day that Travis finally
appeared in Georgeanne's drawing room for a morning call.
He stopped in the doorway, one eyebrow raised, apparently
in surprise at so much company, and surveyed the room.
Georgeanne sat *tête-à-tête* with an impressively bosomed
matron and only turned for a moment to give him a restrained
smile and then continued her conversation with the matron.
Dilys was seated on a sofa with old Lord Daventry, who,
as Travis watched, possessed himself of Dilys' hand and
pressed an ardent kiss upon it. She blushed and gently pulled
her hand from his grasp. There were two young sprigs of
fashion hovering, and at her shoulder Lord Cleveland, who
bent to murmur something in her ear. She cast a laughing
glance up at him, her gray eyes flashing brilliantly, her lips
curving sweetly over her neat, shining teeth.

Travis stood for a moment transfixed. Why, he thought
with amazement, the child is quite presentable, after all. Then
he realized he was staring, tugged at his waistcoat, and turned
away to greet his hostess.

He bowed before her and she held out her hand, which
he brushed lightly with his lips.

"Good morning, Travis," she said, some reserve still in
her voice, for she had still not quite forgiven him since their
quarrel.

"Good morning, Georgeanne. I need not ask how you are,
for I can see plainly that you are very well. I hope you can

reassure me that Harry and all your splendid brood are the same?''

This came from his mouth as a foreign language to Georgeanne, and for an instant she gaped slightly with bewilderment. She could never have imagined Travis— *Travis*—making such a speech, to even refer to Harry by name! It was the first time he had ever acknowledged her husband's existence to Georgeanne.

At last she pulled her thoughts together and replied, ''They are all very well, Travis, thank you. Lady Appleby, allow me to present my cousin Lord Travis Gallant to you.''

Lady Appleby's eyes widened apprehensively, but she bravely offered him her hand. She had clearly heard of him. He solemnly bent to kiss it, somewhat more lingeringly than he had Georgeanne's, and Lady Appleby looked flustered but gratified. He smiled wickedly at Georgeanne before excusing himself with a murmur about greeting his other cousin.

Georgeanne felt only a moment's pang, as any woman would, as she realized that Travis had finally decided to be finished with his long attachment to herself. She very much hoped she knew the reason, but with Travis, one could never be quite sure of anything. He may just have grown bored with continuing to pretend to himself that he was in love with her, or he may have fallen genuinely in love with some young woman and a betrothal loomed, or he may have just set up a new mistress with whom he was besotted.

Travis strolled across the room and stood before Dilys. ''Well, cousin, I see you have little need for more company. Rather an *embarras de richesses*, or perhaps an *embarras du choix* would be the more appropriate phrase.''

Dilys, though till now unaware of his presence in the room, turned from Lord Cleveland and smiled, her eyes wide and steady upon him. ''Good morning, Travis. I had quite given you up.'' She held out her hand and he bent to kiss it.

"I suppose you are only one of a host who have done so, but as you see, the bad penny turns up when least expected."

"I expect you gentlemen know each other?" Dilys said. The gentlemen nodded to each other.

"I had no idea you and Miss Bryn were cousins, Gallant," Lord Cleveland said, sounding less than overwhelmed with gladness at the news.

"Oh, yes, we played pirates together when barely out of leading strings." Travis laughed.

"You and Georgeanne played pirates," Dilys said tartly. "I always had to play the captured foe and be tied to the mast while you two brandished swords and swashbuckled about threatening me."

"Oh, surely we did not always tie you up," protested Travis, grinning.

"Well, I remember once you allowed me to walk the plank you had rigged up in the hayloft. I fell quite three stories into a pile of straw. It is a wonder I survived."

Lord Daventry, apparently feeling one more very young man was the final straw, rose to make his farewells, and Travis quickly possessed himself of the seat next to Dilys, much to Lord Cleveland's chagrin. The two sprigs merely looked wistful.

"Are you enjoying your Season so far, cousin?" Travis inquired.

"I like meeting so many people. Alun and Caroline had always the same people about them. I care rather less for always having to change my gown and have my hair redressed. Men have things far easier in such matters, I think."

"Oh, I don't know," he replied lazily, casting a glance over the two sprigs. "Some spend far more time upon their wardrobes than most women, I believe." One of the sprigs blushed fiercely over his elaborately tied neckcloth, which held his collar points so high he could barely move his head. The other turned away abruptly, perhaps to protect his monstrously padded morning coat with its huge pearl buttons from the gaze and possibly scathing comments of Lord Travis Gallant.

Dilys hastily began to speak of Mrs. Montague's "breakfast" of the day before, which began at three in the afternoon and went on so long she had been forced to miss Lady Mogg's at-home and barely returned home in time to dress for the Foloyts' dinner.

"It all sounds the most appalling bore," Travis drawled. "I don't know how you can bear it at all."

"Why, I notice that you are present at a great many of these occasions," she retorted.

"Never more than one a day, child. One must learn to discriminate. Will you be attending the Austerlys' ball tomorrow?"

"Oh, yes. I am so looking forward to it."

"Perhaps I am not too late to request a set?"

She looked at him in amazement. "But I thought you detested—" She saw his brows come together in a frown and she quickly said, "Yes, of course you may. Which will you like?"

"The last before supper, supper, and the first after," he said promptly, his brow clearing.

"Very well," she said agreeably.

Lord Cleveland, who had been listening impatiently all this while, interrupted to say, "But, Miss Bryn, I had asked you before if I might take you down to supper."

"So you did, sir, but I had not given my answer, and since Lord Travis is my cousin, I feel I must allow him his way this once."

"I'm hanged if I can see why," Lord Cleveland grumbled.

"My lord, I am sure you are very kind to want to take me to supper after having done so the past two evenings," Dilys replied pleasantly.

Travis' lips twitched at the simplicity of her answer, politely pointing out as it did that Lord Cleveland had no rights of possession and was greedy into the bargain. He rose. "I must bid you good morning, cousin."

"Surely a very short visit, Travis?"

"Ah, but I have not the stamina of your youth. Too much socializing in one day plays havoc with my complexion. I will see you tomorrow evening." He bowed to her and to the gentlemen and withdrew to cross the room to bid Georgeanne a brief farewell and then was gone.

Well, thought Dilys, and if she had but known it, Georgeanne was saying the same thing to herself. It was another three-quarters of an hour and several more callers before they could exchange views privately.

"In my opinion he has at last begun to grow up," declared Georgeanne when she had heard all about his words with Dilys.

"How do you mean?"

"Well, he has given up his adolescent infatuation for me, for one thing."

"Oh, no. How can you say so?"

"He inquired after Harry's health. A sure sign. Since we have been back, he has pretended that Harry did not exist, much less the children. He inquired of them also."

"But Georgie, he did stand godfather to Daisy."

"Ah, yes, but I had to plead with him to do it for my sake and for our old friendship and all of that. He certainly did not do it willingly. Still, that may have been the beginning, though he would not acknowledge it."

Dilys felt as though a large boulder had rolled from her heart. She knew she would love him always and had accustomed herself long ago to the fact of his love for Georgeanne. She had not begrudged it to Georgeanne, but somehow it made her feel almost light-headed to think that love was no more. It must be so if Georgeanne said it was, for she always knew these things.

Dilys hurried up to her room. If she were quick, there would just be time to enter this morning's interesting events in her diary and write to Mlle. before they must change to go out again.

Mlle. had called only a few mornings ago and at a moment when Georgeanne was out of the room told Dilys that she herself had corrected the proofs of Dilys' book, thinking it imprudent to send them to Dilys, and that the book should be in the shops very soon.

Dilys had felt a flash of excitement. She had almost forgotten about the book in the heady stream of events that had overtaken her since she had finished writing it. She had not read it since sending it to Mlle. and now felt curiously separated from it and even had difficulty remembering what all she had written in it.

She felt eager to read it again, though she was afraid she might find it very childish and be ashamed to have written it. She had, on several occasions, probed Mlle. as to her feelings on the subject, but Mlle. had been smoothly evasive, saying only that she was quite sure of two things: that it was grammatically correct and that Mr. Conklin would not have printed it if he had not thought it would sell.

She wrote now to ask if Mr. Conklin would send a printed copy to Mlle. as soon as it was ready and, if so, would Mlle. send it along to her immediately. She sent a footman with the note and told him to wait for a reply.

Mlle. wrote back that she was sure that Mr. Conklin would send her a copy, but she very much doubted the wisdom of sending it to Dilys. Lady Brinton might find it odd of her

to be sending such a book to her former pupil, but Dilys need
not fret, for she was quite sure Lady Brinton would waste
little time in acquiring the book for herself and then it would
seem natural that Dilys should request to read it. She, Mlle.,
hoped that Lady Brinton would not find it in any way
unsuitable for so very young a girl.

Dilys almost became hysterical with giggles at this. To
have written a book that might be found unsuitable for herself
to read. Dear Mlle.

10

I have finally—and definitely—settled on my pink for tonight. I have spent most of the afternoon trying on every ball gown I have and became so frustrated and confused I very nearly had the headache. Miss Poore at last said she preferred me in the pink and I was so tired I decided on the instant to wear it and think no more about it. She also suggested that I have a lie-down since I was looking quite tired, so I did and slept about an hour and now feel completely relaxed and calm. He will probably not even notice what I am wearing in any case.

When she appeared in the Austerlys' ballroom, she was wearing sea-foam green despite her earlier resolution for pink. From the square neckline of the tiny bodice her bosom rose as round and white as peeled apples. The skirt of gauze over a stem of darker green silk fell straight from the very high waist tied with silver ribbands. Green and silver ribbands were expertly entwined in her hair. She felt the green was, after all, the wiser choice, and was grateful to Georgeanne, who had suggested it. The gown was definitely more sophisticated than any of her others, and was the only green in the room so far, while pink was everywhere to be seen.

She glanced about casually, but *he* was not there. Of course, he would probably not appear until very late. She hoped he would arrive in time for their dance before supper. What if he forgot! It would be so entirely like him to do so that she wished very much she had never had such a dismal thought. Just the possibility would spoil the first half of the evening, and the eventuality would spoil the second.

All these thoughts passed through her mind as she followed Georgeanne to a sofa against the wall. No sooner were they seated than the two young dandies of yesterday's visit presented themselves to request dances, followed by a positive rush of other young gentlemen of her acquaintance, including Lord Cleveland, who had already made his claim for the first and another after supper.

Then Georgeanne poked her with a warning elbow and she looked up to find Caroline and Alun bearing down upon them. Her face fell in dismay at seeing them. The young gentlemen eyed their approach nervously, then bowed and melted away.

"Dear Georgeanne, how nice to see you. Perhaps I may just sit down. Such a crush on the stairs. Where can all these people come from? The *ton* was used to be much more selective. I must say I saw more than a few that I would hesitate to allow in my own drawing room," prattled Caroline, plumping herself down beside Georgeanne, who hastily shifted away to give her more room. "Good evening, Dilys."

"Caroline, Alun," said Georgeanne politely. "This is a surprise. I somehow had the impression you did not care for balls."

"Dear Lady Austerly—so pressing one could not refuse her. We do not dance, you know. We shall just look on for a time. Or at least I shall. I expect Bryn will retire to the whist room." Caroline's voice held what seemed to be a command in it, for Alun bowed at once and went briskly away, happy, it seemed, to receive his congé.

"Well, Dilys," Caroline went on, "one hears of you everywhere. Perhaps a bit too much, if you know what I mean."

"No, Caroline, I do not know what you mean," replied Dilys.

"Perhaps just a little more discretion. It is not a good thing to be the subject of gossips."

"Discretion? I am not aware of having done anything indiscreet," Dilys said calmly. "Pray do tell me what they are saying."

"Oh, I did not mean to imply anything—well—unseemly," protested Caroline.

"What did you mean to imply?" Georgeanne asked, joining the fray.

"Really, how you both do jump down one's throat," cried Caroline in injured tones. "I implied nothing. Nevertheless, I think you must agree that it is not a good thing for a young girl's name to be too much on everybody's tongue."

"In this case you may rest easy. Dilys is pretty and new. Naturally people will speak of her, as they do of anyone new. They will stop speaking of her when the next new thing comes along. In the meantime, she has only to continue to behave as beautifully as she has until now and give them nothing more titillating to put their heads together over than her newness on the scene."

Caroline sniffed and turned away while Georgeanne turned to wink at Dilys, who grinned happily at Georgeanne's complete rout of Caroline.

Caroline suddenly exclaimed, "Oh, there is my cousin Henrietta!" She waved her fan vigorously at a young woman, who turned away hastily pretending not to have seen Caroline. "Now, there is a pretty girl for you. And such a lovely gown, is it not, Georgeanne?"

"If you care for ruffles," Georgeanne replied dryly.

"But so—so *comme il faut* for a young girl. And while we are on the subject, I feel it is my duty to say that I cannot approve of the gown Dilys is wearing. I do not think it appropriate for young girls to wear low-cut gowns."

"While *I* think it is only young girls who should," replied Georgeanne tartly, raising a significant eyebrow at Caroline's vast and much overexposed expanse of bosom. Caroline turned a dull red from bodice to forehead and began to fan herself vigorously. "Ah, Lord Cleveland, how lovely," Georgeanne cried, turning to greet the gentleman as he appeared before them.

Lord Cleveland bowed over the two older ladies' hands before turning eagerly to Dilys. "I believe the orchestra is just about to start the first set, Miss Bryn. May I lead you out?"

Dilys rose to take his arm, happy to leave Caroline to Georgeanne, who was more than a match for her. She always looked forward to dancing with Lord Cleveland, who was charming in just the acceptable degree. His flirtatious remarks were always delivered in a tone that reassured her of his intention only to amuse and to be pleasant. Tonight, however, there seemed something more pointed in his lovemaking, something serious, she thought, glancing up at him nervously when he said, without a trace of lightness in his voice, "You have quite captivated my heart, fair one."

"Ah, your heart is easily captivated, then, sir," she responded, laughing.

"No, quite the reverse," he said firmly, not smiling back, but looking intently into her eyes.

She turned her head away and changed the subject pointedly. Lord Cleveland was too much a gentleman to persist. He thought that perhaps she was too shy and embarrassed for such a conversation on the dance floor.

He was resolved to think of some way to get her alone, for the most amazing thing had happened to him: he had fallen in love at last! He was eight-and-twenty and twelve years older than his love, but he thought that a very good thing. A girl so young needed the guiding hand of an older, more experienced man. His heart nearly melted with love as he contemplated her innocence. It was as a clean slate upon which to draw the perfect picture of love. Oh, he would teach her of love. Yes, by the Lord Harry, he would marry at last and surprise them all!

Dilys was unaware of the fate being decided for her by Lord Cleveland, and by now she had also forgotten her uneasiness at his sudden descent into seriousness during their dance. She was, as usual, enjoying herself very much with her usual variety of partners, and beneath it all was the tiny void that held only expectancy and was untouched by all the flirting and dancing and laughter and music. It would only become part of the whole when Travis arrived. If he came at all . . . But no! She would not allow herself to think of that.

Then, suddenly, he was there, bending over Georgeanne's hand before turning to survey the room. He had not seen her yet. She ducked her head below her partner's shoulder, shy at the thought of meeting his eyes. The set ended and she was led back to Georgeanne, and Travis was waiting to claim her for their dance. She drew herself up and forced herself to look calmly up at him, smiling and greeting him as she always did, hoping he would assume that her breathlessness was due to the dancing.

The set was half over before she really recovered herself. She had reacted violently to his hand grasping her own and felt as though she moved in a mist where sounds were muted. She must have been replying sensibly, however, for she gradually became quieter inside and could see that he wasn't looking at her strangely. In fact, he was quizzing her in a kindly, almost avuncular way.

"I suppose you are breaking hearts right and left and will finally be led up an aisle littered with prostrate beaux."

"Beaux! I have only dancing partners, and as for breaking hearts, I am not the type who is considered a heartbreaker," she said, laughing and flashing her dark-gray eyes up at him suddenly, forgetting shyness and nerves. "I do not think I will 'take' this first Season at all. Poor Georgeanne, I am sure she had hoped to get me off at once, but I have had no offers, unless you count old Lord Daventry. But then, he proposes to everyone in turn, so I am told. What is it, Travis? Am I talking too much? Why are you looking at me in that way?"

"Oh, I . . . Nothing. I was only thinking of that old court card, Daventry." But he had only this moment discovered that she was beautiful. He had thought of her always as a plain little girl, and more recently as passable and not so plain as he had been used to thinking her, but never had he noticed the brilliance of her fine eyes, the loveliness of her smile, the purity of her complexion. They were not things that one noticed at once and said to oneself, There is beauty, but once one began to notice, one was doubly struck by the discovery and felt one had discovered a Botticelli that every one else scorned as a daub. She was not pretty in the accepted sense, but all her qualities added together became beauty.

"He is very sweet, really," Dilys said, "and pathetic, poor thing. I imagine he is very lonely."

"Now, what can you know of loneliness?" he teased.

"Much more than you, my lord, and firsthand also. I was alone from eight years until only a month or so ago."

"But were you not with your brother and his wife all that time?"

"Yes," she said simply, but with so eloquent an expression in her tone that he could not help laughing.

"I think I understand you. Of course, I am very little acquainted with your brother, but the little I know of his wife I detest."

"Yes," she said, again agreeably, and again he laughed.

They went on together very well after that. The set was over too quickly, but since he was to take her down to supper and have the first set after, she was happy. They sat down to table with Georgeanne and a party already formed, and it was very gay, everyone seeming bent upon being amused and amusing, and again the moments flew. Presently they were back in the ballroom and the music, a waltz, was struck up. Never had a waltz been more magic. She was sure her feet never actually touched the floor. If only it need never stop . . .

When it did stop at last, she looked up at him dazedly and said, "Oh." He laughed and she was embarrassed and said to cover her confusion, "I thought you detested dancing?"

"So I do, as a rule."

"But you dance so well."

"I was well-taught, but to enjoy it depends upon one's partner, and—" But he stopped abruptly and held out his arm. She took it and he led her back to Georgeanne. Once there, he bowed, thanked her politely, and strolled away.

Well, thought Dilys somewhat indignantly, he might have finished his sentence. It was rude, really, not to say he enjoyed it, for I know he did. When she rose to stand up with her next partner, she saw him near the door with Lord Cleveland. They both seemed to be watching her. She turned her head away, but she wished very much she could know what they were talking about.

In fact, Lord Cleveland, in a state of euphoria because of a decision just reached, was being indiscreet.

"You may congratulate me, Gallant, for I will soon be a married man, a state I never expected or desired for myself."

"Oh, yes?"

"I suppose everyone had decided that I was a confirmed old bachelor by now. I thought the same thing myself. Never felt the inclations to leg-shackle myself, imagine you feel the same, since you've never married. I have enjoyed my single state, my brother has sons to carry on the line, all that sort of thing."

"But now?"

"Ah, now, by George, I have met the girl I could bear to spend my life with. Didn't think so at first. Didn't even think she was very pretty, though a nice little thing. And then, before I quite knew what had happened to me, I found myself head over ears in love. Nothing for it now, you see, but to marry her."

"And is she willing, do you think?"

Lord Cleveland smiled smugly. "Oh, I think so, yes. I have not asked her yet, of course. I must move very slowly on this, I believe, for she is very innocent and terribly young and must not be rushed."

"Am I to know who the lucky young lady is?"

At this, however, Lord Cleveland became aware that he was allowing his excitement to loosen his tongue too much. "Oh, I really must not say. All in good time, my dear fellow, all in good time."

However, Travis had not been unaware that Lord Cleveland's eyes were very actively following one figure around the room, and that figure was Dilys. Impertinent, boasting ninny, he fumed. How dare he think that just because his fancy had fixed itself on a girl he had only to snap his fingers. Dilys would never have such a smug, self-satisfied creature as this. I will forbid her to accept him!

He nodded coldly and, turning abruptly on his heel, left the room and the house. He walked along the dark, deserted streets of London, striking lampposts with his cane savagely and fuming impotently. For, of course, he had no rights in the matter at all. Lord Bryn might forbid, but certainly would not, Cleveland being a considerable catch. Even Georgeanne had the right to forbid, but would not if it was what Dilys wanted. But he . . . he had no rights at all.

11

An entire week has passed since the Austerlys' ball and we have not seen Travis once. He was not at the Crofts', the Pride-Galtsons', the Saxbys' balls, nor at Lady Pemberton's musicale—not anywhere! Nor has he called. Most gentlemen call the morning after a ball if they have stood up with you twice and taken you to supper. Or at least send a bouquet—usually both. Georgeanne suggests he may have gone out of town, perhaps on business, since he has several estates, but I think it is just his usual rudeness. Either that, or he has taken me in disgust, and since Georgeanne says he is no longer in love with her, he sees no reason to seek us out anymore. Or, most likely of all, he has taken a new mistress who never lets him out of her sight. I could not blame her, but, oh, it is a melancholy thought. I had hoped he had given over being a rakehell.

Lord Cleveland, meanwhile, had been assiduous in pressing his attentions upon her. He was very much present at all the social events listed in Dilys' entry above. He called every morning and sent a bouquet every day. In fact, he made it quite clear to the *ton* that he was seriously attempting to attach Dilys' affections, and they were the subject of much gossip and speculation.

Lord Cleveland was not an overly proud man, nor a conceited one, but nor was he unreasonable. He knew very well that he was not considered an ill-favored man in face or form, that he was a sensible, well-intentioned, well-educated gentleman who paid his debts promptly, held his wine well, and conducted his amorous adventures with superb discretion. All of these qualities, plus a title and wealth, made him preeminently eligible. It was true, as he said to Travis, that he had never been tempted to marry before, since he thoroughly enjoyed his life as it was and had no interest in changing it for the sake of producing children. His younger brother had three sons already, and one of them would do very well for the next Earl of Cleveland when the time came for it.

Now all those feelings were changed. He very much wanted to marry Dilys and produce a whole nursery full of children. He could not conceive of any reason why, being so eligible, he should not marry her. He realized that she was not the sort of girl to be swept off her feet, he would not love her as he did if she were. There was something in the clear steady gaze of those gray eyes that warned him to go slowly, but he felt confident that steady wooing would produce the desired results. She would come eventually to the realization that she loved him. She had already shown a decided preference for his company.

He was aware that they had become the subject of talk, but he did not mind that. It was nothing but curiosity, really, not based upon any ill conduct on either of their parts, so there was nothing malicious in their gossip. There might be envy on the parts of some young women and their mamas who had entertained hopes, but those hopes had never been encouraged by himself.

He was feeling more than usually optimistic today, for he had finally persuaded Dilys to come out for a ride in the park in his carriage, suitably chaperoned, of course, by his coachman, his tiger, and a footman. He wished they could have been more private, but knew it would be hopeless to suggest such a thing. Still, he would have her to himself away from all those ever-hovering young blades who were eternally present when he called, and away from the avidly interested eyes of the *ton* in the drawing rooms and ballrooms. Of course, there were bound to be interested eyes in the park also, but at least they could not overhear everything they said to each other.

He arrived early to pick Dilys up and was shown into the drawing room, where Georgeanne sat alone, all the morning visitors having departed and Dilys gone to change for the drive. Georgeanne greeted him warmly, causing his hopes to be reinforced. She would be a strong force in any decision made by Dilys. They sat chatting amicably until Dilys appeared. She had changed into a fawn-colored pelisse over a white muslin walking dress and a small poke bonnet in fawn trimmed with pale-blue ribbands and a small white curling plume in front.

Once settled in the open barouche, Lord Cleveland complimented Dilys upon her costume.

"I will convey your kind words to the one who deserves them," Dilys replied lightly.

"Your dressmaker?"

"No, indeed! Darling Georgeanne deserves all the credit, as she does for all my gowns. I am only beginning to develop taste."

"Oh, my dear Miss Bryn, surely—" he began to protest laughingly.

"No, no, it is true," she interrupted, "you see, until I was eight, I had no interest in clothes. And after that, until Georgeanne came home, Caroline—my brother Alun's wife, you know—dressed me, and she has no taste at all."

"Nevertheless," he pursued, determined to make her the object of his compliment, "the gowns without the, ah, presence of the wearer would have no meaning. They must become the wearer, bring out her own best features, as this costume does for you. I have never seen you lovelier.''

''Oh, well—'' She broke off in some confusion, turning away from the warmth of his expression. She saw that they were objects of a great deal of interest now they were on the Row, which swarmed with carriages, riders and those on foot enjoying the early-spring day and the opportunity of showing off new costumes, new equipages, or a recently purchased pair of matched carriage horses.

Progress was slow in such dense traffic, and added holdups were caused by carriages pulled up side by side while the passengers greeted one another and exchanged gossip and pleasantries, oryoung gallants astride held up carriages to make their compliments to pretty girls. The sunshine, the fluttering muslins and silks, the bright colors, the sound of laughter and light talk, all created a festive air that was in every way agreeable to Dilys despite the interested eyes turned her way and her nervousness about the growing seriousness of Lord Cleveland's attentions. She was determined not to acknowledge her awareness of this and hoped her offhand manner would, at last, discourage him. It had been so much more pleasant in the beginning, when he had flirted so lightheartedly.

''My dear Miss Bryn, may not I have just a small bit of your attention?'' Lord Cleveland said, somewhat plaintively, recalling her wandering thoughts. ''I have looked forward so eagerly to this day when I might be alone with you for once.''

''Alone?'' She waved her hand to indicate the throngs about them and laughed.

''Yes, well, as alone as it is allowed us to be. Society makes it impossible to be more so.''

''Oh, but why should we want to be? It is so gay here,

with everyone laughing and looking so happy and at their best.''

''I have no interest in 'everyone,' '' he replied, looking directly into her eyes, ''only in the someone who sits beside me. The world would be well lost for me did it contain only you.''

She blushed furiously at so direct a declaration and looked away—directly into the bleak stare of Travis driving a dashing high-perch phaeton slowly past in the opposite direction. Their glances locked for a moment before he looked sharply away. Before they passed completely, she caught a glimpse of the young lady seated beside him, a vision that etched itself upon her eyeballs down to the last detail of ribband trim upon her gown.

Dilys noted a lack of chaperon, not even a tiger up behind to lend some aura of respectability, and came to the conclusion that this could not be a lady, or at least not in the accepted terms that denoted at the very least friends to guard her reputation. Her heart sank, for the girl was so beautiful: masses of auburn ringlets, alabaster complexion, slanting green sparkling eyes, perfect profile, and a very full pink mouth set off with a delicious dimple in the left corner.

Lord Cleveland, unaware, continued his ardent protestations, which Dilys, sunk in misery, did not hear. At last the thought that they might circle about and repass the same carriages caused her to turn and say, ''Please, my lord, I find I have the headache—perhaps too much sun. Could I ask you to take me home now?''

Completely nonplussed at such a response to his words of love, he could only stare at her for a moment before leaning forward to give orders to the coachman. They drove back to Brinton House silently and, once arrived, had little to say beyond apologies from Dilys and solicitude for her health from Lord Cleveland. Dilys slipped quietly up to her room and, carefully turning the key in the lock of her door, threw herself upon her bed, pulled a pillow over her head to muffle her sobs, and indulged in a good cry, which finally did give her the headache she had so falsely claimed.

Meanwhile Travis drove on in grim silence, the picture of Dilys' sparkling eyes and rosily blushing face taunting him with her evident happiness at the words being so earnestly addressed to her by Lord Cleveland. He did not delve into the question of why he should feel himself taunted by such a sight, but only let his temper grip him and send his eyebrows plunging together in a scowl of displeasure.

"Well, I vow, my lord, if you are going to just sit there looking as cross as two sticks and never even notice me, I might better have stayed at home with Mama. She at least speaks to me," said the lovely creature at his side with a pout of her luscious lips.

He started, causing his horses to break stride, and by the time he had settled them he was able to turn back with a semblance of pleasure to Miss Elizabeth Hayes. Under his undivided attention her reproachful look soon disappeared and she was all giggles and prattle again, flashing her dimple provocatively at him, especially when any other young gentlemen were by to observe, for though not overburdened with brains, Miss Hayes had well absorbed her mother's lesson that it never did to put all one's eggs in a single basket.

Actually, Miss Hayes was registered at birth as Eliza May Haypole, but Mrs. Haypole had felt this had a too rural, not to say cloddish, sound, and she had changed the name upon moving to London. This move had occurred after Mr. Haypole had deserted hearth and home in the company of an actress with a touring troupe passing through the village. Left with only ten pounds, thriftily saved from her housekeeping money, and an eighteen-year-old daughter of staggering beauty, Mrs. Haypole had decided to invest her assets where she had some chance of an equitable return, and moved to London. There she threw herself upon the mercy of a childhood friend, Margery Fox, a seamstress who timidly advertised herself as Madame Reynard, Couturière, who not only took them in, but was persuaded by Mrs. Hayes, as she now called herself, to make up several costumes suitable for a young girl about to launched into the London *ton*, spending some of her remaining ten pounds for the fabric required.

Needless to say, the *ton* proved elusive to such as Mrs. Hayes, but before many weeks had passed she met a jolly lady come to Margery for fittings on a new evening gown. She was a Mrs. Wilson, who admired Elizabeth wholeheartedly and talked much of her own dear daughters, Harriette, Amy, Fanny, and the baby, Sophia. She finally invited the Hayes to dinner to meet them.

The evening arrived and Mrs. Hayes, convinced she had met a very fine lady and was now on the road to a wealthy husband for Lizzie and comfort for herself, set off in high fettle with her daughter. The sumptuous meal and the good-natured company, who accepted them naturally, was followed by an influx of young gentlemen as the evening progressed, all Lord this or that or heirs to Lord thus and so, until Mrs. Hayes' head reeled with triumph. Here was vindication indeed for all her privations and suffering, for surely one of these elegant gentlemen buzzing around Lizzie like bees about a plate of honey would inevitably become her son-in-law. She looked upon all of them with the misty eyes of prenuptial maternal love.

She kissed Mrs. Wilson's cheek fervently when they departed at the end of this delightful evening, amazed and grateful for the kindness of the woman and her daughters, who did not seem to be at all put out by Lizzie's beauty. Which was certainly unusual, considering they were not in the least pretty girls themselves. Still, they must have something to draw all those titled and surely wealthy young men to them.

It took her some weeks and a number of carefully veiled innuendos by the sadly repressed Madame Reynard before Mrs. Hayes understood exactly what that draw was. Here was no member of the *ton*. Far from it. Mrs. Wilson's daughters would never be accepted into respectable drawing rooms however often they went to the play or the opera on the arm of a titled young gentleman. After further discreet inquiries she doubted they would be accepted into the front parlors of people of their own class. Mrs. Haypole's small-village soul felt a momentary flash of outrage at such unbridled licentiousness as was accredited to this family. Why, they were the scandal of London!

But very soon her more practical side came to the fore. She knew no one else in London, and should she throw the Wilsons over, there would be an end of all those wealthy and titled prospective sons-in-law. For Mrs. Hayes had no idea of selling *her* daughter's charms for anything less than marriage.

So she continued to visit Mrs. Wilson and encouraged interested young men to call upon herself and her daughter in Madame Reynard's front parlor. Not being up in the ways of her betters, she quite often found excuses to leave her daughter alone with an infatuated young man in case the lad wanted to propose. Miss Elizabeth reported a number of proposals, but none of them for marriage. Mrs. Hayes was indignant but not discouraged. Surely one of them could be brought up to scratch with time.

She had great hopes for the latest of these, Lord Travis Gallant, who had lounged into Mrs. Wilson's drawing room one evening late and seemed quite taken by Lizzie, though Mrs. Hayes noted he was still there when everyone else, including herself and Lizzie, had taken their leave, and from the casual arm he laid about Harriette's waist as they bid them good night, she suspected he stayed the night. This did not worry Mrs. Hayes. Men would be men, and there was no fear Lord Travis Gallant—or any of the rest, for that matter—would ever propose marriage to Harriette Wilson.

He might, however, propose marriage to Lizzie if they both played their cards right. Mrs. Hayes had impressed upon Lizzie the need for the utmost propriety. No casual arm about *her* waist, no stolen kisses, no liberties at all with her person. Ladylike flirting was allowed, of course, and every encouragement to give him reason to think he had attached her affections. If possible, encouragement to express his feelings in letters, which might come in handy at a later date if his ardor cooled.

And had she not been proved right in her precautions? For here he was nearly every day in Margery Fox's front parlor, and escorting Lizzie to the play and the opera and giving her grand suppers with champagne and a gold bracelet, and taking her to race meetings and giving her his winnings. All of this and never, according to Lizzie, making any improper proposals, much less taking any liberties with her person. Surely the man was serious in his intentions. Why else, otherwise, would he be wasting his time? Mrs. Hayes' hopes were very high.

Poor woman, with all her native shrewdness, she was not to know that gentleman with honorable intentions would never have behaved toward a young lady of good family in any of those ways so esteemed by Mrs. Hayes, except perhaps for the last about not making improper advances.

12

Yesterday was my seventeenth birthday and I feel many
more years than one have passed since my last, which
Miss Poore and I celebrated alone with a cake
smuggled up to the schoolroom from Cook. So much
has happened to me since that I feel more like one-
and-twenty than seventeen. Georgeanne and Harry
gave me the most heavenly diamond earrings and Miss
Poore a pair of lavender kid gloves and the little boys
pooled their money and gave me a kite! So adorable
of them. We are to take it to the park and fly it this
afternoon.

Lord Cleveland, during his usual morning call, learned
of this expedition as well as the reason for it and begged to
be allowed to join them. Harry came in and, hearing his
request, declared that he would come also, whereupon
Georgeanne decided to be of the party.

They set off in two carriages, Georgeanne and Dilys with
the little boys and Harry with Lord Cleveland, and avoiding
the Row, with its traffic, they found a deserted grassy knoll.
It was a perfect day for kite-flying with light winds and sun
and shadow as whole battalions of cottony clouds were
herded across the pale-blue sky. The little boys, pushing and
shoving and giving contradictory orders, took charge of
Dilys' kite and struggled mightily to get it off the ground
while it dipped and sailed and fell time and again. Harry had

found, in the attic, an old but much larger kite from his boyhood and he and Lord Cleveland had it sailing aloft in no time at all. The little boys one by one deserted Dilys for their father's more exciting game, leaving Dilys and Georgeanne to struggle on alone. At last, however, they got it up and were laughing and shouting so enthusiastically that the boys returned and begged to be allowed to fly it. The sisters give it over into their charge and sat down breathlessly upon the grass to watch the men and boys' exertions.

"Lord Cleveland is so nice," Georgeanne said presently. She waited for some response but none was forthcoming. "Do you not think so, Dilly?"

"What? Oh, I beg your pardon, dearest, did you say something?"

"I said Lord Cleveland is very nice," Georgeanne repeated patiently.

"Oh. Yes—yes, he is."

"What were you thinking of while your mind was so far away?"

"Oh, nothing. I really cannot remember." Another silence ensued. "Did you know Travis has a new mistress?"

Georgeanne thought, Aha, but she only said, "No, I had not heard. How do you know?"

"I saw them driving together last week in the park."

"How do you know it is his mistress?"

"Well, they were quite alone—not even a tiger or a footman."

"I see. That was the day you got the headache when you went driving with Lord Cleveland, I suppose?"

"Yes—yes, I believe it was."

Again Georgeanne thought Aha, but only said, "Ah, well. Oh, Johnny, do be careful," as little Johnny, running after his older brothers, tripped and fell, then leapt to his feet as though nothing had happened, and ran on. "I wonder if little boys even notice when they fall down? Mine never seem to. What a perfectly heavenly day you choose for your birthday. I wish mine were in the spring instead of gloomy old November.''

There was no reply to this remark and Georgeanne noticed that Dilys was again staring into the distance, her expression depressed. Presently, however, the men turned both kites over to the boys and came to fling themselves down on the grass, and Dilys turned to them and began to talk and laugh as though all was as right with her as with the day.

When they piled into the carriages for the return home, Dilys somehow found herself in Lord Cleveland's carriage with the two oldest boys. Johnny, the baby, rode with his parents, sitting on his mother's lap.

During the drive Lord Cleveland produced a small package and handed it to Dilys. ''For your birthday, if I may be allowed,'' he said.

The boys clamored excitedly, for they loved all presents, but they subsided disinterestedly when, upon unwrapping, it proved to be ''only a book.''

It was a small volume of Byron's poems bound in white leather. Dilys, though pleased with the volume, was dismayed by the gift, for it was just the sort of gift a young girl would be allowed to accept from a young man to whom she was not affianced, and it would be unduly prudish and discourteous to refuse it or even to protest. At the same time, however, to accept it seemed to her to forge a stronger link in her acceptance of his courtship. Her thank-you was subdued and uncertain-sounding.

The boys exchanged the congratulatory look of those whose gift had been clearly more pleasing, having been greeted with cries of joy and spontaneous and delighted hugs and kisses for all of them.

Back home at last Harry pressed Lord Cleveland to return

for dinner. "Only family for once, thank the Lord. Oh, and
old Pryce up from the country, but you won't mind him,
I know. Dear old chap."

Lord Cleveland assured Harry he would not mind old
Pryce in the least and accepted with pleasure.

Miss Poore, looking very nice in mauve silk and flushed
with excitement, was the object of Sir Wicklow's attentions
throughout the dinner and afterward in the drawing room.
Georgeanne sat down at the pianoforte and played and sang
a number of pieces to entertain her guests. Dilys, an
indifferent pianist with no singing voice at all, firmly declined
to follow her, but Miss Poore was at last prevailed upon and
played competently and sang in a surprisingly pleasant
soprano and was much applauded.

Harry compared her voice favorably with a singer
presently appearing at the opera, and this inspired Lord
Cleveland to invite them all to be his guests on the following
evening at the opera, with supper afterward. Everyone but
Dilys entered enthusiastically into this proposal. She
mentioned the musical evening at Lady Hobbs to which they
had a long-standing invitation.

"Oh, there will be such a crush no one will miss us,"
declared Georgeanne, "and this will be much more fun, and
certainly better music, for I know the quartet she has engaged
and they are second-rate, and she confessed to me herself
that she could not prevent the Harrison sisters from
volunteering to sing some duets."

Dilys, who had heard their dreadfully arch and usually flat
renditions in Caroline's drawing room and had limned them
faithfully in her book, shuddered with distaste. Harry, who
had also heard them before, declared that no power on earth
would persuade him to expose himself knowingly a second
time to the Harrison sisters. It was at last settled that they
would make up a party for the following evening as Lord

Cleveland's guests. No one looked more delighted at the prospect than Miss Poore, unless it could have been Sir Wicklow Pryce.

When the guests were gone and the family had retired, Georgeanne in her dressing gown went along to Dilys' room and found her sitting back against her pillows reading a slim, white, leather-bound volume by the light of a candle.

"What are you reading, dearest?"

"Byron's poems. Lord Cleveland gave it to me on the way home this afternoon for a birthday gift," Dilys said, handing her the book.

"Well, how very pretty it is, and most appropriate."

"Yes, I suppose so, but I wish he had not done so," said Dilys doubtfully.

"My dear, I assure you the book is entirely acceptable as a gift to—"

"Oh, I know that. It is just . . . Well, I wish I had not to accept it, is all."

Georgeanne patted her hand. "Accepting such a small token of esteem is not a committal, Dilys."

"No, of course. It is only that he might think, you know . . . And a family party in his private box at the opera and . . . Well, everyone already thinks . . . I can see it in their eyes when we are in public together and I do not want . . . Oh Georgie, would you think it dreadful of me to cry off tomorrow night with the headache or something?"

"Not dreadful, darling, of course, but I do hope you will not do so. You see, if you do, Miss Poore will be bound to insist upon staying behind with you, you know she will, and I very much want to give her this treat, especially as Sir Wicklow is to be of the party."

"Sir Wicklow? But what—"

"Oh, goose, do you suppose romance is only for the young?"

"Romance? Why, Georgie, do you really think—"

"Well, I *hope*, let us say. And there are indications. I doubt he has been to London more than once a year since his wife died twenty years ago. He comes for business and leaves when it is finished. According to Harry, he detests London. Yet, here he is again, not a month after he came for your party. He wrote Harry he was coming, which he has never done before. Why should he do that if he was not angling for an invitation? And he is very attentive to Miss Poore. I plan to have the wedding from here, and you and I will attend her and Harry will give her away and the older boys will usher and Johnny can be ringbearer. I have been thinking about her wedding dress and I believe it—"

"Georgie, stop!" Dilys cried. "Why, they have met but twice and you have their bridal planned to the last detail. For heaven's sake, are you mad?"

Georgeanne looked at her, puzzled. "I do not see what is so mad about it?"

"Oh, Georgie," Dilys said, and began to giggle and then could not stop. The more she thought about it, the funnier it became. Presently Georgeanne could not help laughing herself.

"Well," she said at last, wiping her eyes, "I suppose I am becoming dotty with the thrill of matchmaking. Just the same, you must come tomorrow if only to indulge me in my madness, lest in my frustration I take to raising bulldogs and going to race meetings like that dreadful Lady Crane, who smokes cigars."

Faced with such an alternative, Dilys was forced to concede with as good a grace as she could muster and duly found herself seated between Georgeanne and Miss Poore in Lord Cleveland's private box at the opera on the following evening, the gentlemen seated behind them. She was very much aware of the many pairs of opera glasses trained upon the box, and was sure the female heads leaning together were discussing the imminence of an announcement of her betrothal in the near future.

She forgot all this when she discovered that one pair of glasses were raised to the eyes of Caroline, seated in a box across from them with Alun and another, quite elderly couple, accompanying them. Or rather Alun and Caroline must be doing the accompanying, for Dilys knew quite well that neither of them cared for opera and were much too closefisted to pay to see it.

Dilys allowed herself to become quite animated and waved and smiled before leaning to Miss Poore and pointing out Caroline with a large gesture. Miss Poore, speaking over her shoulder to Sir Wicklow, turned, smiled, nodded to Caroline, and turned back to Sir Wicklow before Caroline could turn away from her greeting with an indignant flounce. Only Georgeanne and Dilys were witnesses, and were much amused.

This incident reconciled Dilys somewhat with having to be where she did not wish to be, and she settled down to enjoy the first act despite the solicitously hovering presence of Lord Cleveland behind her. During the interval they strolled up and down in the corridor and Dilys hoped very much for a closer encounter with Caroline, but she did not appear. When they returned to their box, Dilys noted that Caroline was still seated with her hostess and did not look their way even once.

Then, just before the second curtain, as the house was settling down in antipation, there was a stir in the box beside Caroline's. All eyes turned in that direction and a beautiful young girl tripped forward to the railing of the box, laughing and talking over her shoulder to her escort, still in shadow at the back of the box. Her auburn curls glinted in the candlelight into an aureole about her lovely face, her perfect shoulders and considerable amount of bosom rose like fine glowing marble from the froth of deep-blue gauze about them.

There was an audible buzz from all over the theater that rose in volume as Lord Travis Gallant stepped forward to her side. He stared around arrogantly, and when his eyes met Dilys, he bowed. Dilys forced a smile and nodded to him, looking back calmly, though a trembling seemed to have seized her entire body as she recognized the girl she had seen with Travis in the park.

Georgeanne, raising her own glasses now, said, "What a monstrously pretty creature that is! Good God, there is Travis. Oh, oh, do look, Dilly, look at Caroline!"

Caroline had leaned forward to peek around the barrier that separated her box from the one next to her, a simpering smile already fixed in place, convinced that the late arrivals causing such a stir could only be royalty. When Travis saw her, he immediately took the girl's hand and turned her and clearly introduced her to Caroline to the edification of the entire house. Caroline gaped in slack-jawed astonishment, too shocked to react quickly enough to draw back before such an insult could be completed. When the girl curtsied, Caroline at last drew back and turned her back ostentatiously —and much too late. The deed had been done, and Travis was grinning wickedly as gusts of mirth shook the audience. Oh, what a rare *on-dit* to pass along during tomorrow's morning calls upon those so unfortunate as to have missed the event.

Dilys was grateful that the curtain rose almost immediately, for despite a moment's amusement at Caroline's discomfiture, her own feelings were in danger of overcoming her composure as a dumb misery settled down in the region of her heart. She concentrated upon the stage, swallowing back the tears she was determined not to allow, and somehow managed to pull herself together. She also resolutely refused to allow her eyes to stray away from the stage even once. When the curtain descended, she was nearly reduced to tears again, this time with gratitude, when Harry declared he was devilish hungry and had had enough singing for one evening. The other two gentlemen agreed and Dilys rose with alacrity and made for the door. The other ladies followed her and soon they were away.

Georgeanne was well aware of Dilys' unhappiness, but knew that any sympathetic word or gesture would undo her completely, or even any acknowledgment of awareness would be disastrous to her sister's precariously restrained feelings. She therefore chattered away vivaciously throughout the meal that followed, to cover Dilys' lapses into silence, and succeeded so well that all the rest of the party were very gay and convinced they had never spent a more enjoyable evening. Even Lord Cleveland was deceived.

Miss Poore, flushed with attention and the glass of champagne pressed upon her by Sir Wicklow, became quite animated and told a story amid gales of laughter of Caroline's one and terribly humiliating encounter with royalty when she was presented at the Queen's Drawing Room and had curtsied so profoundly she had tipped over backward and sat down upon the floor and had had to be hauled to her feet by the gentleman usher.

Dilys made herself laugh with the others. After all, she scolded herself, what had she expected? That a waltz with herself would change the leopard's spots?

13

I have resigned my hopes, which I now realize were childish and unrealistic in the extreme. I feel mortified at my own naïveté in thinking I had any chance to affect Travis' life. He has been perfectly content with that life for years now, and if, along the way, his conscience pushed him into showing kindness to me, it proves my own gullibility that I allowed myself to build dreams of rehabilitation on his few moments of attention. I shall now repudiate all such infantile fancies and concentrate upon a new novel. I wish the Season were already finished and we could retire to the country and the solitude I crave. I shall never marry, so it is pointless to continue this fruitless round, which is all about finding a husband.

Though this entry sounds rather contrived, even pompous, and certainly confirmed her youth in its eagerness of renunciation, it was sincere. However, though she was heartfelt in her wish to retire from London, and Lord Cleveland, it was unfortunately, or fortunately, impossible for her to suggest leaving to Georgeanne and Harry, who had been away from London and all their friends for so many years. It would be pure selfishness on her part, and Dilys could not even allow herself to look unhappy or discontented lest she spoil their pleasure. So she went about to parties and balls and dinners and paid visits and received callers with

Georgeanne as she had always done, and put a brave face upon her unhappiness.

She was in the drawing room with Georgeanne several mornings later when Caroline was announced. Lord Cleveland had been and gone, but two young gentlemen still lingered. Caroline stared at them so pointedly that after a few moments they nervously rose and took their leave, as Caroline had meant them to do.

"Goodness, what a bore for you to have your drawing room cluttered with such creatures as that," she said, settling herself more comfortably upon the sofa.

"Oh, not boring at all. We enjoy company," Georgeanne said mildly.

"Neither of those young men has any fortune and, being both younger sons, will never inherit any, so if you are hanging out for a proposal from either of them, Dilys, I hope you will take my advice and set your sights higher."

"I am not ha—" began Dilys indignantly.

Georgeanne cut in. "Did you enjoy the opera, Caroline?"

"Not particularly. I am not partial to music."

"But one meets interesting people," Georgeanne said provokingly. She would never have teased Caroline ordinarily, but when she attacked Dilys, Georgeanne forgot her manners.

"I do not find it so. And since you have brought up the matter, I must say I think it is unwise of you to encourage someone in Miss Poore's position to aspire to hopes beyond her station."

"Her station?" Dilys gasped, again indignant.

"What do you mean, Caroline?" Georgeanne said. "She is your cousin, is she not?"

"Very distant—many times removed. But we do not acknowledge her socially. We look after her, of course, since she is penniless, but her mother ran away with a music teacher and her own family repudiated her. However, that is by the way. The fact is that she is no better than a servant."

"She is a gentlewoman," Georgeanne reminded in a steely voice.

"Her mother was. Nevertheless, she has worked for wages most of her life," Caroline sniffed.

"Wages? Do you tell me you paid her wages? Or that any one else in your family did so?" Dilys asked angrily, for she knew very well that it was not so.

"We clothed her and sheltered her and gave her her food!"

"And used her as a servant. However, she remains a gentlewoman and may aspire as high as she pleases," said Georgeanne.

"I think you will find that Sir Wicklow Pryce is higher than she can fly," Caroline retorted spitefully.

"Well, you are entitled to your opinion, of course, as I am to mine. In the meantime, they have met but three times, and I do not feel Miss Poore can be accused of having any aspirations at all so far, so this discussion is premature."

"Would your aspirations regarding Lord Cleveland also be premature?" Caroline asked archly.

"Yes! I do not—" began Dilys, but again Georgeanne cut her off.

"I suppose you refer to Lord Cleveland's aspirations. Naturally, there are no such aspirations on my part, even less on Dilys'. She has just celebrated her seventeenth birthday, however, so we do not quite despair of her being left upon the shelf as yet."

"Well, for all that, all London is gossiping about how she has set her cap for him, with your encouragement," Caroline cried.

"If that is so, Caroline, you, as her sister-in-law, should refute such allegations indignantly," Georgeanne returned coolly. "Now, gratified though we are that you found the time to spare to call upon us, I am afraid we must be very rude. We have another engagement and are already, I fear, much later than is polite. I know you will forgive us if we bid you good morning." She had risen as she spoke and was crossing to the door. Caroline had nothing to do but follow her and, with a cold nod by way of farewell, sail out the door Georgeanne held open for her.

Georgeanne closed the door upon her and collapsed against it, laughing helplessly.

"Oh, Georgie, how can you laugh? She will never forgive us, and she might do anything!"

What Caroline did was have herself driven home in a barely contained rage and send off a missive inviting Sir Wicklow to call upon her on the following morning. She had learned, she wrote, of his arrival in London and having heard so much of him from her dear father, Lord Thomas Dudham, would welcome meeting him.

Sir Wicklow was much flattered, and replied that it would give him the greatest pleasure to attend her. He was more than a little puzzled, however, for rack his brains though he might, he had no memory of ever meeting anyone by the name of Dudham. He was not sure who she was exactly, though he supposed he must have met her at some time. He did not connect her with Dilys.

He duly appeared on the Bryn doorstep the following morning and was shown into the drawing room. "My dear Lady Bryn, how kind this is of you," he said, advancing to kiss the hand she extended.

"My pleasure, dear sir, indeed it is. Dear Papa spoke of you so often I felt we should meet."

"Yes, your father, I cannot quite—"

"Alas, dead these many years. However, we will not dwell

upon that sadness now. I hope you are enjoying your stay?''

"Oh, yes, enormously. I—"

"You live in the country, I understand. Do you plan to return there soon?''

"Well, in a few days, perhaps. I am finding this visit so pleasant," he said, and then looked rather surprised at having successfully completed a sentence.

"Yes, of course. Actually, you were pointed out to me several nights ago at the opera. You were with the Brintons and my sister-in-law.''

"Your sister-in-law?''

"Miss Bryn. My dear husband's sister.''

"Oh, I see. A delightful young lady. Of course, Bryn—I confess I had not made the association. Yes, yes, quite delightful. I enjoy her company vastly. And the dear Brintons, too, of course.''

"And the servant?''

"The servant?''

"Yes, the other lady of the party. She is Lady Brinton's servant.''

"Oh, no, indeed. That lady is Miss Poore, a friend who resides with the Brintons.''

Caroline laughed airily. "Oh, my dear sir, I fear they have not been quite honest with you. Perhaps they hope to get her off their hands by finding her a husband. She is my sister-in-law's governess, you see.''

Poor Sir Wicklow became somewhat nervous. He could not like the lady before him, despite any friendship he may have sustained with her father. There was something venomous in her tone and there was a hard and unlovely look in her eye. He began to speak determinedly about the opera and the vocal qualitites of the various performers. That topic exhausted, he began upon acquaintances they might share in common, and carrying on, as he was aware, in a boringly garrulous way until he felt his duty done, he rose, still prating away at a great rate, barely giving her time to respond, made his farewells, and escaped. Leaping into his waiting carriage as though all the furies were after him, he ordered his coachman to take him back to his hotel quickly. Once there, he drank down a brandy to restore his equanimity.

Poisonous woman, he thought in a calmer frame of mind. Up to some mischief, I'd stake my life on it. Must make sure I don't have any further encounters with her, no matter who her father was. Dudham—Dudham—damned if I ever knew a Dudham.

Much restored, he sat down at his writing table and penned a note to Miss Poore asking if he might have the pleasure of taking her for a drive on the following day.

Miss Poore's feelings upon receiving this missive may well be imagined. She twittered about her room in an excess of nerves for quite half an hour, stopping every few moments to reread the note to make quite sure she had understood it correctly. She found it impossible to believe that such a distinguished gentleman as Sir Wicklow Pryce could truly seek her company in this way, despite the kindness he had shown her on their previous meetings. They had, after all, been in company and he was the soul of courtesy. It never, even for a moment, entered her head to suppose he could have any particular regard for her. He was simply an old friend of Harry's family and it was natural he should seek him out when he was London. His kindness to her was only what he would extend to any member of Harry's household. But this . . . this seemed to go beyond that. She simply did not know what to make of it and at last sought out Georgeanne and with trembling fingers handed her the note wordlessly.

Georgeanne read it quickly. "Well, how delightful, Miss Poore. Shall we just step upstairs and look at your wardrobe to decide what you will wear?"

She swept Miss Poore back to her bedroom and began flinging various gowns and pelisses upon the bed, chattering away about their suitable and unsuitable qualities, until finally she chose a pale-green silk and a darker green silk pelisse to wear over it and moved on to bonnets, Miss Poore the while twittering helplessly about her trying to express her confusion about the propriety of accepting the invitation.

At last Georgeanne said, "Oh, nonsense, Miss Poore! He is a lovely man. You have nothing to fear, I assure you."

"My dear Lady Brinton, I would never dream of imputing any evil intentions to—"

"Besides," Georgeanne interrupted, "he does not drive himself, so there will be a coachman there. No, I do not care for any of these bonnets. Wait, though, I have the very thing and it will suit you perfectly. I will just fetch it."

She darted out of the room and returned in a few moments bearing a Milano straw poke bonnet. Miss Poore still stood in the middle of the floor where she had been left.

"Sit down, Miss Poore, and you will see how right I am," Georgeanne said, and led her to the dressing table and pushed her onto the seat before it. The brim was lined with a pale-pink silk and the same silk tied it under the chin. It did become Miss Poore very well. "There now, you see, quite perfect. I was sure it would be."

The next day in the early afternoon Miss Poore was to be seen seated beside Sir Wicklow being driven by his coachman at a leisurely pace through the crowded roads of the park. She was twittering inside, but managed to maintain a sweetly calm demeanor. The lovely Italian straw bonnet did much to brace her courage, for she felt very fine in it. Women always feel in better spirits when they are wearing something new, even if is only something new to them.

Sir Wicklow kept up an entertaining commentary as they

drove along, telling her the various histories of people passing who were acquaintances of his, while she smiled and asked questions and exclaimed and enjoyed herself very much and quite forgot to be nervous.

It was while she was laughing gaily at one his stories that they passed Caroline driving in the opposite direction with several of her sons beside her. Sir Wicklow bowed to her and Miss Poore nodded and smiled. Caroline stared in disbelief for a few seconds, then drew herself up, much affronted, and deliberately snubbed them.

Miss Poore felt herself blushing with shame at such rudeness. After a small silence Sir Wicklow said, "Do you know that lady, Miss Poore?"

"Oh, yes, but it seems she will not know me, though we are cousins, several times removed."

"Cousins, you say?" he exclaimed, astonished.

"Yes. That is how I come to be with the Brintons. May I tell you of it?"

"If you care to do so, my dear Miss Poore, I should be honored," he replied gallantly.

Thereupon Miss Poore told him about herself and her lowly position in Caroline's family, leaving out none of the unsavory details, such as the impecunious musician who had married her mother and abandoned her and her child, as well as her mother's struggle to raise her daughter alone after being turned away by her family, and finally of her mother's death and her own childhood as an orphan in Caroline's mother's household, scorned by all and forced to wait upon her cousins to earn her bread.

She told it all without self-pity, and when she had done, she stared straight before her, her head raised stiff and proud while a silence developed. Then she felt his hand warm upon her own held tightly together in her lap.

"My poor child, what a wretched time you have had, to be sure. Why, you must have a backbone of steel to have risen above all that so courageously."

She turned her face slowly, almost disbelievingly, toward him, to find his eyes glassy with tears. At that sight a low sob, quickly caught back, escaped her despite all she could do, and she turned quickly away.

He patted her hand and cleared his throat. "Well, now, in exchange for that confidence, I must tell my own tale, though I fear you will find it fearfully dull after *your* adventures. Now, where shall I begin? Well, when I was a lad—oh, perhaps of twelve or thereabouts . . ."

14

It is the most ravishing spring I have ever seen, almost heartbreaking in its perfection—or it would be so, were my heart not already broken. Such an odd phrase. I wonder where it first arose? Naturally, the heart cannot actually break, being of soft matter, but mine literally feels that way, with jagged bits sticking out to tear at the surrounding flesh, creating actual pain. I must remember the reality of this pain for a book. It is something I know of, which is what Mlle. says I should always write about. It astonishes me at times when I am thinking clearly that after all these years of loving him with no expectation of anything, I allowed two dances and a few kind words to turn my head so completely that I began to dream of the impossible. What a fool I am! I shall learn better, of course, being still so young, and I shall recover, I suppose, from this "illness," but I find little consolation in that thought now.

Dilys' abigail interrupted this melancholy entry to announce that Lord Cleveland waited below to take Dilys driving. She rose reluctantly to allow herself to be helped into her pelisse and bonnet. She had wanted very much to refuse this invitation, but could not bring herself to be rude by just saying no, and could think of no reasonable excuse. Apart from that, she felt, guiltily, that she had no right to refuse. After all, had she not welcomed his company and his flirtation at first? Had she not shown a clear preference for his company, however safe she had thought herself to be in doing so? The fact remained that she had used him for her own amusement and owed him something, however unpleasant the consequences turned out to be. It was clear that, mysteriously, he was not in the least discouraged by her offhand disregard for his most ardent declarations.

Had she but known, her seeming disregard, which he interpreted as innocence, only enamored him the more. He was convinced her youth had protected her from such declarations before, or kept her ignorant of their meanings. Her confusion and blushes when he became too forthright he attributed to the child's mind only slowly reacting to the hitherto unknown realm of love. She was, for him, the pure, green bud slowly opening in the warmth of his ardor.

Today he had given his coachman orders to take a less public road through the park before they entered the Row, for he had made a plan to get her apart from all other ears if only for a few moments in order to more nearly approach a proposal. They had gone only a short way along this road before she noticed the new way.

"What is this, my lord? Do we not drive on the Row today?"

"Oh, indeed we shall, Miss Bryn, but I thought a less-frequented route would give us the opportunity to enjoy the loveliness of the day. The trees are in their first green. I don't know about you, but this my favorite time for trees, when they are so young and fresh-looking."

"Oh, yes, indeed. I love to see them so," she sighed.

"Ah, I knew it!" He leaned forward and ordered the coachman to pull up. The footman leapt down to open the door and lower the steps, and Lord Cleveland stepped out and held out his hand to her. "Come, Miss Bryn, let us walk along for a bit and enjoy this beauty at a more leisurely pace.'' She only stared at him with her great gray eyes and did not move. ''Come now,'' he said with a coaxing smile, ''I am sure you will enjoy it of all things, just as will I.''

She allowed a long, uncomfortable moment of silence to draw out before she said firmly, ''No, Lord Cleveland, I do not believe I will, if you please.''

He felt a momentary flash of irritation with her for exposing him to this refusal before his servants, which he found humiliating. But only for a second, then his habit of mind to attach all such denials on her part to her innocence reasserted itself, and he forgave her. The darling girl had never walked apart alone with a gentleman and would not do so without the sanction of a chaperon. How good it was that this was so. Ah, she was adorable!

He jumped back into the carriage. ''Just as you please, dear Miss Bryn. How right you are, no doubt the ground is damp. Drive on to the Row,'' he ordered the coachman. He saw that he must apply to Lady Brinton before he confronted his love with such a decision in future.

Dilys was delivered home again at last, grateful to be there, and more grateful still not to have encountered Travis with his new love. Grateful also that for once there was no affair to attend that evening. She sent down word that, being much wearied, she would not come down to dinner and would like instead a tray in her room.

This brought Georgeanne at once to see what was the matter. She fussed about worriedly, though Dilys assured her she was not ailing, only tired. Georgeanne pulled a chair up to the chaise longue where Dilys lay in her dressing gown. ''Now, then, tell your old Georgie what is wrong,'' she said quietly, reaching out to capture Dilys' hand and lay it against her cheek.

''Oh, darling Georgie,'' Dilys cried with a little gasp as she caught back a sob that rose involuntarily at the love expressed by Georgeanne's gesture. She swallowed hard, however, and managed a shaky smile, her eyes glistening with unshed tears she hoped Georgeanne would not notice.

Georgeanne noticed everything. "Did you see Travis again today on your drive?" she inquired casually.

"No, but nearly everyone else one has ever met seemed to be there—staring and—and smirking. But before that, we went a different way and there were no other carriages about and Lord Cleveland wanted me to leave the carriage and walk with him and I would not and . . . Oh, Georgie it was horrid."

"Why, darling girl! I am so sorry. I should never have allowed you to go. You have been doing too much and I—"

"Now, do not try to make it your fault, Georgie. I have only myself to blame that things have come to such a pass."

"What blame? What pass?"

"Oh, for having allowed Lord Cleveland to think that I . . . It was all so much nicer in the beginning. Why did he have to change?"

"Well, my darling," said Georgeanne, who was beginning to see the problem, "he has fallen in love."

"But why?" Dilys demanded unreasonably.

"My love, that is a question no one has ever been able to answer. What makes one person more attractive to us than any other on earth? Do you not often see couples together and wonder what could have drawn them to each other? Look at Alun and Caroline, for example."

"But what shall I do?" Dilys cried.

"Why, just do not accept to drive out with him or to dance with him so often."

"Would that not be churlish after, well, being his friend when I thought it was safe to do so?"

"Well, then, you must just let him propose and refuse him."

"But I do not want him to propose. I could not bear it!"

"Silly goose, how can you refuse unless he does? I agree that having encouraged—no, not encouraged—allowed this passion to develop, it would be unkind just to rudely turn away from him as though you were tired of him. There is no way out, you see, but to allow him to propose."

This disagreeable advice was not at all what Dilys had hoped to hear. Just what she had hoped for Georgeanne to tell her she did not know, but since Georgeanne was usually right, Dilys had reluctantly to concede that she must be right in this. For, of course, it was impossible to refuse what had not yet been offered, and the longer she refused to allow him to make the offer, the longer she would have to suffer his lovemaking. Really, a woman had no way of halting the process, especially when one's lover seemed not to notice one's discouragement of his suit. And in this case, the friendship that had seemed so lacking in danger had changed so gradually into something else she had had no chance to halt before it was too late and the peril upon her.

Georgeanne watched her sister and came close to guessing everything she was thinking. Poor baby, she thought, I wish she did not have to be unhappy, but it will not hurt her in the end. Georgeanne used some very unladylike language in her thoughts regarding Travis, but did not for a moment believe that everything would not come out as she had decided it should.

"Oh, I forgot to tell you, Sir Wicklow called while you were out to tell us that he is returning to the country."

"Oh! Oh, dear—was Miss Poore—"

"She was there, and not looking in the least unhappy. I can only suppose everything in that quarter is still well. She was so serene that I feel sure they had discussed it already. He asked me to bid you good-bye for now with his devoted

regards. Now, what shall you wear to the Dacres' ball
tomorrow night?''

After her retired evening and a quiet day to follow it Dilys'
spirits were much restored and she felt equal to the Dacres'
ball, even though it included her usual two dances with Lord
Cleveland. Supper she had been careful to grant to one of
her other partners. She wore a gown of a glowing rose color,
made up from the silk Georgeanne had brought her from
India, and looked, she thought, as well as one with so few
claims to beauty could do.

The Dacres' ballroom had one entire wall of French
windows, and tonight, due to the unusual warmth of the
season, they all stood open upon a ballustraded terrace with
steps leading down into a garden hung with fairy lights. Itw
as all very romantic and Dilys tried to think herself back into
the mood of her first few balls when, though in love with
Travis, she was not entertaining any unrealistic fantasies
about him and had been able to enjoy every moment. Aided
by the knowledge that it was not in the least likely he would
appear tonight, not having come to anything for several
weeks, she succeeded to some extent. She even managed to
laugh and exchange quips with Lord Cleveland. After their
dance he returned her to Georgeanne, and when her next
partner came to claim Dilys, he remained and seated himself
beside Georgeanne.

"The Dacres have the perfect setting for a ball, to my
mind," he commented.

"Yes, it is very lovely. Though really best suited for this
kind of weather. I should imagine it might be difficult to heat
in the winter. But, then, I cannot ever remember their giving
a ball in winter. Perhaps that is why."

"Yes," he said agreeably, though clearly with other
matters on his mind.

Good heavens, thought Georgeanne in a momentary panic,

is it possible he is going to ask my permission to pay his addresses to Dilys?

Not exactly, she realized when he said, "I wonder, Lady Brinton, if you would think it permissible for me to invite Miss Bryn to walk on the terrace during our next dance. It is so very warm I do not think she could possibly take a chill and she would enjoy seeing the lights in the garden, I think."

"The decision must be entirely her own, Lord Cleveland. I have no objections. In fact, if Harry comes before the evening is over, I shall get him to take me out. I should quite like to see the lights myself."

"Perhaps you would do me the honor of joining Miss Bryn and myself . . ." he began with automatic politeness and a sinking heart.

She laughed. "No, no, sir. I would not dream of being such a spoilsport."

So it was that when he came to claim Dilys for their second set, he led her out only to suggest she might better enjoy a stroll on the terrace. She looked startled, and because he felt sure she was on the point of refusing, he hastened to reassure her that he had obtained Lady Brinton's permission before making the suggestion.

She was not best pleased by this, but realized resignedly that it was as well to get any unpleasantness, thus she characterized poor Lord Cleveland's proposal, behind her. Georgeanne was right, she could not refuse until she had been asked. Naturally, she could not be positive he would ask her tonight, but a walk upon the terrace alone with him, even though there would surely be other couples taking the air, was as near alone as he was likely to get, and he would also realize that. Indeed, he had surely already realized it, why else to ask her and arm himself with Georgeanne's permission first?

So, bracing her shoulders bravely, she nodded and turned

with him toward the terrace. It was truly very beautiful, the air so soft and balmly as to seem tropical, the fairy lights glimmering among the fresh greenery most alluringly. There were several couples walking up and down the terrace, but many more strolling about the neat graveled paths of the lawns and shrubberies.

Lord Cleveland led her slowly toward the far end of the terrace, which was deserted at the moment. He turned to the balustrade and gestured toward the gardens. "It is very pretty, is it not?"

"Yes, very pretty."

"I am so glad we are here—together—at such a perfect moment. It could not be a more ideal setting for what I want to say to you. Perhaps you may guess what that may be?"

She swallowed her rising panic and, looking directly into his eyes, said, "No, my lord. I do not know."

Adorable creature, he thought rapturously. How grave and steady she is, as trusting as a child. "I hope, however, you have by this time come to understand my regard for you."

"We are—friends, my lord," she said, feeling a perfect idiot, for it was all such a farce and she had to allow it to play itself out, even if it meant telling lies like not knowing what he wanted to say to her. But what was she to do? Say, Yes, I know what you want to say and the answer is no? What if that was not what he was going to say, but instead ask her if she preferred the waltz to all other dances or Beethoven to Bach?

"Indeed, we are friends, my dear Miss Bryn, and to begin as friends is the best way in the world to lay the foundation for a more important relationship. I hope you will agree, my dear—my very dear Miss Bryn." He waited, looking eagerly into her eyes to see the dawning of understanding there.

At last she turned her eyes away, but was constrained to reply, though with somewhat pedantic carefulness, "I agree that friendship is a necessary basis for any relationship."

"Exactly, my more than dear one," he cried softly, reaching for her hand. "I knew you would understand me. My feelings for you have overcome every obstacle I could put in their way, until at last I must speak of them. I love you, dearest girl, and beg that you will allow me to speak to your brother."

"Oh, please do not! Indeed, my lord, you must not," she cried in great distress.

"But, my darling Dilys—may I call you so?—it is only proper that I seek permission before I ask you to be my wife," he said with a gentle little laugh, as one would when instructing a child.

"I cannot . . . I regret very much . . . Oh, I wish you will not say another word of this. It is impossible," she said in great agitation.

"Be calm, my little one, be calm. I understand. It is natural that one so young and innocent should be thrown into a confusion by her first declaration. We will not rush the moment." He patted the hand he still held, and she, having forgotten he was holding it, now snatched it away. Another couple came slowly toward them and she turned away from him to stare out into the garden.

How badly I am handling this, she thought miserably. I cannot allow it to go on. She waited until the couple turned and went back the other way before she turned and faced him squarely. "I am sorry, Lord Cleveland. I know you do me great honor, but please do not go on. It is impossible."

"Ah, my princess. How brave and beautiful you look when you are serious. I have taken you by surprise. Perhaps I have been too precipitate. I will give you all the time in the world to accustom yourself to the idea. I know you will—"

"No. No, I will not, my lord. It will never be possible."

"Never can have but little meaning to one so young. Be

assured, my dearest, my love will wait for you.''

"Do not wait, my lord. I could never marry you. I do not love you as a woman must love the man she marries.''

"I am confident you can know nothing of love as yet, my darling. When you become more at home with the idea—''

Stung to exasperation by his refusal to hear her, she blurted out, ''I know a very great deal of love, my lord. I fell in love when I was nine years old, and I love him still and always shall. I could never love anyone else.''

He stood frozen in shock, the words ''love him still'' and ''always shall'' echoing hollowly inside his head. How was this possible? His green bud, his tender shoot, saying these words. It could not be! He was horrified, revolted by the idea that she could ever have loved, could still love, anyone at all. Where was the innocence that he had been so confident of, that he had loved her for? His picture of her slowly crumbled to dust, and with it his love. Too shattered to speak, he held out his arm and, when she laid her hand upon it, led her back into the bright, crowded, noisy ballroom and directly to Georgeanne. With a profound bow to both ladies, he turned and left.

15

Well, I allowed him to propose, and I do feel better that it is over, though I wish I had managed it with more dignity. He was so obtuse and, at last, to force him to understand that I was serious in my refusal, I simply blurted what I thought never to admit to anyone. Of course, I did not say whom I loved. I feel very guilty about Lord Cleveland, but Georgeanne says I must not, since it will only serve to depress my spirits and give him no comfort at all. And if, knowing of it, he should take comfort, he would not be worthy of it. I think often now of how I shall get through the rest of my life, which seems to stretch so emptily and joylessly into the future. When I feel that way, I go to the nursery and play with Daisy, and that comforts me. So I have decided that I will concentrate on being a good aunt to darling Georgeanne's children, and try to become a really good writer, and look forward to all the adventure and romance of India—for I know Georgeanne will never go and leave me here alone. I even look forward to it, knowing I will be on the other side of the world from Travis and so unaware of what he is doing. While I am here in the same city, even in the same country, I shall always be wondering and hoping.

Even as Dilys was writing this entry in her diary, Travis, in a dark-red brocade dressing gown, was cutting into his breakfast beefsteak. The hour was near midday, but a late night over the cards had kept him abed until now. As he raised the first bite to his mouth, his butler entered the room.

He waited in stately dignity until Travis had swallowed and looked up before announcing, "There are two, er, persons wishing to see you, my lord."

"Well, what do they want?"

"They would not say, my lord."

"Tell 'em to go away."

"I did so, my lord, but they, ah, declared they would wait upon your convenience no matter how long it took."

"Male or female?"

"Female, my lord."

"Oh, the devil. Did they give you their names?"

"A Mrs. Hayes and a Miss Hayes, my lord."

"Good God! Well, when I have finished my breakfast, you may show them in."

Some half an hour later, the butler looked in, Travis nodded and in another moment the two ladies were shown in. Mrs. Hayes had a most belligerent light in her eye, but Elizabeth only flashed her dimples in a smile and then became absorbed, gape-mouthed, at the grandeur about her.

Travis lounged back in his chair, his long legs, crossed at the ankles, stretched out before him, one arm hooked over the back of his chair. He did not rise, nor did he offer them a seat.

Mrs. Hayes was much affronted by this rudeness and drew herself up to administer a rebuke, but then decided propitiation might work better than reproaches at this point. "My lord, we worried that perhaps you was took ill or something when we hadn't seen you for such a long time, so I told Li—Elizabeth that we must just come around and reassure ourselves of your health, as good friends must do."

He cocked a cynical eyebrow at her. "I appreciate the kind thought, but I am very well, thank you, Mrs. Hayes."

"I can see that, my lord, indeed I can, and I am very thankful for it. But I felt it were my Christian duty to see for myself."

"Well, now you have seen, madam."

"Yes, well—poor Li—Elizabeth has been nearly fretting herself into a decline, so I thought—"

"I am happy to be able to set Miss Hayes' mind at rest. Now, if you will excuse me, ladies, I have an engagement."

"But, my lord—" Mrs. Hayes gabbled, feeling the situation was slipping out of her control. Then she braced herself and took up the cudgels again. "I think this is a very shabby way to treat your friends who worry for your health and has offered you every hospitality and courtesy, my lord."

"Ah, how remiss of me. Perhaps I may offer you some refreshment?" he said with a sardonic half-bow, for he had still not changed his position.

"Kind of you, I'm sure, but we'll not trouble you, my lord," she said, mollified.

"Then, if there is nothing else—"

A hard light came into her eyes. "Now, see here, my lord, you can't just go a round courting an innocent young girl and then just go away and leave her pining and broken-hearted as though nothing had happened."

"My dear Mrs. Hayes, I fear there are a number of words in your statement I cannot agree with. First there is 'courting,' then 'pining' and 'broken-hearted.' I will reserve judgment on 'innocent.' "

"How can you, sir? You steal a girl's heart and then cast slurs on her good name."

"Steal?" he said incredulously, his eyebrow rising as he thought of the three hundred pounds or so he had given her, not to speak of the trinkets.

Mrs. Hayes flushed, thinking of them also. "Money can't

pay for the unhappiness you caused, making her believe you was courting her, making love to her—''

"Miss Hayes," Travis rapped out suddenly and loudly, causing Lizzie to jump, "did I ever make love to you?"

"Oh, no, sir, you was always the perfect gentleman," she gasped with a fearful glance at her mother. "Truly, Mama," she added placatingly, lest her mother think she had gone against instructions against stolen embraces.

"Hold your tongue, Lizzie," snapped Mrs. Hayes furiously.

Travis smiled, uncrossed his ankles, and slowly rose to his feet and lounged across the room to ring for a servant.

"This has been charming, ladies, but I really must beg you to excuse me now."

"My daughter has been expecting a proposal at any moment. You can't just attach a girl's affections and then drop her as though nothing had happened," cried Mrs. Hayes.

"Nothing *has* happened, Mrs. Hayes, as you have just heard from your daughter's own lips. As for expectations, I believe they are all your own, for, lovely creature though she is, I doubt Miss Hayes has the wits for expectations."

"I'll see you in court for this, sir!"

"You may try, Mrs. Hayes," he said agreeably as the butler appeared in the door. "Show these ladies out, Humbly."

Mrs. Hayes hesitated a moment, but at last threw up her chin and marched to the door, but once there, she realized her daughter was not following and turned back. Lizzie stood staring, gape-mouthed again, at a huge portrait over the mantel, of a Gallant ancestor astride a rearing black horse. Mrs. Hayes marched back, took her by the arm, and snatched her unceremoniously out of the room, hissing, "Idiot girl!" as they passed into the hall.

Travis crossed back to his chair, turning it to the fire, and slumped down into it, his chin sunk onto his chest, glowering from under drawn brows into the flames. His life seemed to him unutterably boring and flavorless. Though he had faithfully followed all the old courses, nothing had any appeal left for him—neither women, nor cards, nor racing, nor hunting.

He had taken up Elizabeth (Lizzie, he thought to himself with a little grunt of laughter) as he had taken up others when Georgeanne had married, hoping her beauty would work some magic, divert his mind from things he did not care to think about. It had worked very well before, but now his thoughts would not be diverted and Elizabeth's inanities, her stupidity, had worked against her beauty to such a degree that he had only found her boring, and left him without the least desire to make love to her. He had continued to be seen in public with her to keep up his reputation, but even that gesture had come to seem empty to him. He simply could not care any longer what anyone thought.

He had been very much aware of Mrs. Hayes' ambitions for her daughter, and had been expecting some word from her when he did not appear for a week in the front parlor of the little modiste where the Hayes resided, and had also known fairly well what her tactics would be. He had had, after all, some experience in that way before. He did not blame them for trying, but he was too wary to be caught like that.

He should, he thought broodingly, have made his position clear at the beginning so that the girl's hopes would not be raised. No, not the girl's, she was too feather-witted to have hopes for more than pretty geegaws and good times. The mother, however, had clearly thought he was in love with her daughter and would marry her. He wished now that instead of being so rude and brusque with the woman, he had set her straight about what she might expect for her daughter if she went on the same way she was going. On an impulse he crossed over to his desk, and pulling paper toward him and taking up his pen, he wrote, rapidly, instructions to Mrs. Hayes, exactly what she should do and should not do if she hoped to find a husband for her daughter. He advised her also to return home and find a good steady village man for the girl, but if she remained in London, to have nothing more to do with the Wilson family if she hoped to save the girl's reputation. He ended by advising her to set her sights more realistically, for he very much feared she would have no luck in finding a lord to marry her daughter. He enclosed a hundred pounds, sealed it up, and rang for a footman to take it around to her directly.

Then, shrugging impatiently, he paced restlessly about the room for some time before calling for his valet to help him dress. He would go to his club. Perhaps his friend Burton would be there, or at least he could have a few hands of whist to pass the time.

He had played several hands before Burton strolled in. Travis rose at once and they went off to drink some wine together in another room. Travis quizzed his friend about his forthcoming nuptials to a girl to whom he had been betrothed for a year, and Burton quizzed him about Miss Hayes and learned of the morning's visit and its result.

"Oh, speaking of betrothals, you're the very man I need," Burton said suddenly.

"I will not marry your sister, Burton, though she is sweet as an angel."

"Fool! You know my sister is married these six months. No, the thing is I have a wager with Coutts about that little cousin of yours and Lord Cleveland. And do you know, I saw him just this morning, face so long it covered his neckcloth, preparing to leave town. Said he'd had enough of London. Now I have bet Coutts she'd never have the fellow and this leads me to suspect she's given him his *congé*. Am I right?''

Travis, whose brows had drawn together forbiddingly at the first mention of his cousin and Lord Cleveland, was now looking at his friend with a very different expression. At last he said, ''I don't know.'' After a moment of staring off into the distance, he turned and started out of the room.

''Ho! Gallant! Where are you going?''

''Why, to make sure you've won your wager,'' called Travis with a laugh as he went out the door.

16

I have heard that Lord Cleveland has left London, and of course there is a great deal of talk and speculation. People one would have thought to have better manners only stop short of asking me outright if it is because I have rejected his suit. It is really disgraceful to be so eager for gossip. When questioned, I profess to be unaware of his movements (as I am!) and pretend ignorance at all insinuations and probings. It is all becoming most tiresome. Apart from that, Harry has been approached twice now with offers from gentlemen who, now the field is clear, feel compelled to declare their undying passion for me. Harry told me of it and I could not put a face to either name! I told him not only to refuse, but to turn down anyone else who applied without referring the matter to me at all as I have no intention of ever marrying.

Not an hour after this entry Dilys was brought word that Lady Bryn was below and wished to see her. Oh, Lord, thought Dilys in dismay, why did I not go to the silk warehouse with Georgie this morning? For a panicked moment she contemplated sending down word that she was ill, but Caroline was capable of forcing her way upstairs to see for herself. No, better to go down and get it over with. Whatever can she want now? Dilys wondered as she tidied her hair. Her stomach churned with nerves at the thought of facing Caroline without Georgeanne there to take the brunt of Caroline's unpleasantness.

"Good morning, Caroline," she said. "I am sorry Georgeanne is not here to receive you. If she had known you would be calling, I am sure she would have stayed in to see you."

"You need not think those missish airs will get you anywhere with me, my girl. I have known you too long to be taken in by them."

"Long but not well," Dilys murmured.

"What is that?"

"You seem in an angry mood this morning, Caroline. What has upset you?"

"Do not pretend with me, Dilys. You know very well what I am here to talk to you about, and why I am upset."

"I am sorry, but I do not," Dilys said firmly. Keep your temper well in check, she admonished herself silently. Do not give her the pleasure of seeing you lose your temper.

Caroline snorted her disbelief in a most unlovely way. "Perhaps it will refresh your memory if I tell you that it has come to my ears that a certain gentleman proposed and was refused by you."

Dilys felt the blood rising in a wave over her face. "I am not responsible for any displeasure you may feel after listening to idle gossip," she replied stiffly.

"I see you do not deny it, madam!"

"I am not required to deny or affirm any bit of tittle-tattle that you may have picked up. I try not to listen to gossip myself."

"Did you or did you not refuse an offer from Lord Cleveland?" demanded Caroline harshly.

"I cannot discuss this with you."

"Not discuss it? How dare you take that tone with me,

missy? I'll not have it, do you hear? Since you do not deny it, I must take it that it is true. I had some faint hope that it might not be so, but I see I am not to have that gratification. Lord Cleveland proposed and you were idiot enough to refuse him. Lord Cleveland! How *could* you be so stupid? You were always the most pigheaded, heartless creature I have known, but I did at least credit you with a fair share of brains.''

"If you have finished, Caroline—" Dilys said coldly.

"No! I have *not* finished. Who are you to turn down such an offer? The Clevelands are as well-connected as any family in England, and all are extremely wealthy. You could not have hoped for a better match if you waited twenty years for it. Where was this precious sister of yours not to have advised you better?''

"Ah, Caroline, you are asking for me?" Georgeanne said from the doorway.

Caroline swung around, her face as red as a turkey cock from the angry diatribe she had just delivered.

"Dear me, you look quite heated, Caroline. Can I offer you some refreshment?''

"No. I am speaking to Dilys regarding her astonishing refusal of Lord Cleveland.''

"Why astonishing?" Georgeanne crossed the room to sit down beside Dilys.

"I am surprised you can ask such a question. Surely *you* know the advantages of making a good marriage,'' said Caroline with a sneer in her voice, for Harry was a very wealthy man.

"Indeed I do. They include love, tenderness, and interests in common. Those were the advantages I looked for and have received.''

"Love! Pah! Good matches are made with connections and means.''

"Well, as I am very well-connected myself and had plenty

of means of my own, I was not forced, as some are, to seek them in marriage. Nor is Dilys.''

"You are talking bubble-headed nonsense! Alun should have been consulted about such an important decision.''

"The decision belonged to Dilys only. Now I think we have said enough on a subject that is, or at least should be, private between Dilys and Lord Cleveland.''

"Lord Travis Gallant, my lady,'' announced the butler from the door, Travis coming in directly upon his heels.

Caroline pulled herself up and looked down her nose at him. Dilys had started at the announcement and now stared at him in disbelief. Georgeanne rose at once and went to extend her hand to him in welcome. He kissed it and crossed to bow to Caroline. She sniffed and turned away, snubbingly. He shrugged and turned to Dilys with a smile.

She smiled back and gave him her hand. His lips warm against her knuckles sent an electric thrill up her arm and caused her heart to thump alarmingly. "Travis,'' she said a little breathlessly, "how nice of you to—to call.''

"I will bid you good day, Georgeanne,'' Caroline said icily, rising and stalking to the door.

Georgeanne followed her to the door courteously. "Good of you to call, Caroline. I hope you will come to see us again soon.''

"Humph!'' Without bothering to lower her voice, Caroline added as she passed into the hall, "I am surprised you allow that scoundrel into your drawing room.''

Georgeanne only laughed as she followed her out and closed the door behind herself.

Travis stood before Dilys, staring down at her silently for a moment, and then said, "I hope you will not think it disgustingly prying of me, but I have heard a certain rumor I hope you will confirm as true.''

"Why should you hope so?'' she inquired in surprise,

staring up at him, her gray eyes large and puzzled.

"Well, I . . . Oh, for many reasons, I suppose."

"What is one of them?"

"One is that I did not think he was good enough for you. I do not care for the fellow."

She wished she could bring herself to ask for the other reasons, but could not do it. In fact, she found she could not think of anything to say at all.

"You still have not answered my question," he reminded her.

"What question?"

"Whether the rumor was true or not."

"It is true."

He smiled. "I am glad. Would you like to come riding with me tomorrow?"

"I do not ride. I have never cared for it."

"Then come for a drive."

"I should be frightened to drive in that carriage."

"Frightened—you? I do not believe it. However, if you are referring to the high-perch phaeton, I did not mean that one. I have several carriages, you know."

"Another, then," she said with a consenting smile.

Georgeanne came back into the room. "What a pesky woman she is. Never happier than when telling other people how they should conduct themselves. Well, Travis, it is good of you to remember that we exist. If we are too boring as company, you might remember you have a goddaughter here whose health you might trouble yourself to inquire for from time to time."

"I felt sure there was no need. All your children look quite revoltingly healthy. You look very well yourself, Georgeanne. Breeding again, are you?"

"Mind your manners, Travis. Where have you been all these weeks?"

"Here and there, Miss Pry, here and there," he said airily.

"Yes. So I have heard. But you were not here, you know. We have missed you."

"Oh, well, I thought it best to stay out of Cleveland's way while he did his courting, since I do not care for him."

"Why, he is a perfectly nice gentleman. What could you find not to like?"

"A great deal," he said darkly, his brows drawing together. "Certainly, he was not good enough for Dilys."

"Pho, pho, pho, sir, and who will be, I wonder?" she said with a teasing laugh.

"Georgeanne, oblige me by going away and tending to your household or something. I want to talk to Dilys."

"Go away! You must be mad, my boy. Besides, I was away, so you have had plenty of time to talk to her alone—more than any other gentleman has been given, I assure you, and only because you are a cousin."

"Then I will go. I do not care for talking with two women at once. Will eleven suit you?" he added, turning to Dilys. She nodded. "Good morning, ladies," he said, bowing, and left the room.

The moment the door closed behind him, Georgeanne turned to Dilys. "Eleven?"

"Tomorrow. He has asked if I would like to drive with him tomorrow."

"Good heavens! Well, that will be pleasant, but your reputation will be in shreds."

"Oh, he has assured me that it will not be in the high-perch phaeton," Dilys said, "so there will be a driver, I suppose, and a footman."

"Oh, yes, certainly, but just driving out with him will set tongues wagging at both ends. His reputation is very bad, you know."

"I do not care in the least. All that clucking and gossiping makes me feel quite ill."

"Oh, I agree it is sickening. Naturally, we will have Caroline around here again when she gets to hear of this."

"He is my relative, more so than is she. Let her come," Dilys said darkly, hoping Caroline would indeed come and hear what she would have to say to her if she dared say horrid things about Travis.

There was a musicale that evening at the Philltons. Dilys kept watch for Travis, but he did not appear. She was content, however, and sat dreaming and inattentive all evening.

She was awake at dawn and went at once to throw open the window to check that it was not raining. She was reassured by the cloudless sky and hung out the window breathing deeply of the cool air, watching the grayness turning rosy, then pale gold, as the sun rose. She was calmed by the sweet quiet of the morning and, kneeling there in the window, laid her head down on her arms and dozed off.

Her abigail found her there when she came with Dilys' morning chocolate, and there was much fussing and scolding about taking chills. Dilys was tucked back into her bed and begged to stay there for at least an hour to warm herself. She was glad to do so, to dream away the time before she could reasonably start her toilette for the drive.

He was a little early, which pleased her; he handed her with suave courtesy into the carriage, making gracious queries about her comfort and bestowing upon her a small posy of violets that lay on the seat. There was a coachman with a footman beside him and two more footmen seated behind the carriage on a bench attached there for that purpose.

Georgeanne, who had come to the door to see them off, raised an appreciative eyebrow at so much chaperonage and gave Dilys a barely perceptible wink. Dilys giggled. Travis climbed in beside her, the footman put up the steps and closed the door, and Travis gave the order to start.

"What amused you?"

"Oh, nothing, really."

"Tell me," he demanded sternly.

"It was Georgie," she said, unable to withstand something in his tone. "She was astonished by so many servants."

"Ah," he said, his voice smoothing out, seemingly satisfied with her answer.

They entered the park and were, naturally, the attraction for hundreds of pairs of eyes, and as they progressed down the Row, crowded as it always was, an extra vibration of excitement seemed to mark their passing. Travis, of course, was always an object of interest, but now Dilys was also because of Lord Cleveland, and together they presented the *ton* with so much to speculate upon they were for once nearly sated and became quite heady, like bees gutted with nectar.

Travis, inured to gossip and stares, seemed not to notice, but for Dilys it was like a punishment. She cringed back, her eyes rooted on her lap.

"What is it?" he asked abruptly, seeing her discomfort.

"They all stare so," she mumbled.

"Put your chin up and smile and stare back," he ordered. "Or will you allow yourself to be cowed by such a crowd of drawing-room dandies and cackbrained old women as this?"

She whipped her chin up and smiled dazzlingly into the openmouthed stare of Lady Dacres, who was just passing by.

"That's the way," he said approvingly, and then began to tell her a story filled with the ludicrous mishaps of a recent race from London to Bath in high-perch phaetons in which he had participated. He soon had her laughing and asking questions and all the time nodding at acquaintances and twirling her parasol gaily.

Once up and down the Row, and then he ordered the coachman to turn off into a byroad, empty at this hour when everyone came to see and be seen on the Row. She relaxed and breathed a deep sigh of relief.

"Oh, come, surely it was not such an ordeal."

"Not now that it is over," she said with a laugh.

"Do you want me to take you home to recover with your smelling salts?"

"I am not a smelling-salts kind of person. I have never felt faint in my life."

"I am very glad to hear it. I have never cared for swooning females."

"Besides, it is much more pleasant here than the Row. So peaceful."

"Would you like to walk for a bit?"

"Oh, do let us!"

They alit and strolled off, but not out of sight of the carriage and the servants. Dilys forgot completely that only a few days before she had refused to walk with Lord Cleveland. All she could think of was the astonishing fact that she was actually here with Travis, that he had come back after she had convinced herself that there was no possibility of it. She could not stop herself from taking little sideways peeps at him just to reassure herself that he was actually there beside her.

Presently they went back to the carriage and were driven on. As they were leaving the park, they saw approaching them in her carriage their relative, Lady Sommers. Both carriages pulled up and they exchanged greetings.

"I have heard a rumor, which, if true, pleases me very much, Dilys," old Lady Sommers said in her straightforward manner.

"It is true," said Dilys resignedly, knowing it was pointless to fence with Lady Sommers.

"I congratulate you on your good judgment," said Lady Sommers. Travis emitted a bark of laughter. "Ah, I see you agree, Travis." She darted a look from him to Dilys. "But then, you would, would you not?" She gave him a wickedly mischievous smile, poked her coachman in the back with her parasol, and was driven away, waving them a perfunctory good-bye.

17

> I am so very happy that it sometimes frightens me. I have to keep telling myself that I must not give way as I did before and begin to entertain any expectations. I must behave to him as my cousin and my friend from childhood who from time to time remembers to inquire after me or show me a kindness, but I must remember that in his very active life I hold only a small and unimportant position. And not only behave so to him, but know so in my heart. Oh, but it is so difficult!

There were several entries, similar in content, in Dilys' diary at just this time, for it was a lesson she was determined to learn perfectly to save herself the pain she had already experienced. It was not easy, now when he was so charming and kind and seemed so determined to ingratiate himself. She was sure, however, that she could deceive him, having learned very well how to hide her feelings during the years she had lived with Alun and Caroline.

The only way, she decided, was to always speak to him as though he were very nearly a brother—just, in fact, as she had always done. On thinking back over their few encounters, she realized she had always been at great pains to hide her true feelings. There had never been anything even approaching a display of emotion, except for the time she had cried when he visited her when she was nine. His reaction had been a pat on the head and a quick escape. She did not blame him for that, as he had been only nineteen at the time, but he had grown, if anything, even more taciturn since then and she had never once felt she had broken through the impenetrable barrier he seemed to have built around himself.

They met several times a week now at balls and parties, or when he paid a morning call, or took her driving, and the *ton*, not slow to notice such things, sat up alertly and observed. Was it possible Travis Gallant was trying to attach his little cousin? The less charitable females professed to be astonished by the attraction the chit had for gentlemen.

"Dozens of proposals, one hears, and all refused, including Lord Cleveland!"

"Pah! I, for one, seriously doubt there was ever such a proposal. He is much too wily and sophisticated to be taken in by that schoolroom air. Why, she isn't even pretty."

"A taking sort of manner, though, and all that money. That would get her all the proposals she could want even if she were a positive antidote."

"Oh, how true. I mean, only think, first Lord Cleveland and now Travis Gallant, neither of whom one ever expected to allow themselves to be caught. Well, I ask you!"

The three matrons whose heads had been close together as they spoke all turned to face the circling couples in the ballroom and trained avid eyes upon Dilys as she danced with Travis.

Dilys was saying, teasingly, "Do you still race to Bath in your high-perch phaeton, cousin?"

"No. I have become too old for such childish tricks as that."

"Goodness! And you still totter about the dance floor quite spryly for one of your advanced years."

He grinned. "Oh, I manage."

"I shall make you a gift of a cane on your next birthday."

"And I shall know where to apply it," he threatened.

"How paternal that sounds. You are practicing for your nursery, I make no doubt."

"How you chatter. I remember you as being such a quiet child."

"Between you and Georgeanne I was rarely given the opportunity to speak. Still, I am flattered you remember me as a child."

"Quiet and skinny, with great staring eyes," he said promptly.

"Very flattering, sir," she said, laughing.

"There has been, ah, some improvement."

"You are too kind," she said, lowering her eyes in a parody of modesty.

"You are never able to pretend missishness. Which is just as well," he added darkly.

Some days later as they were driving in the park, she said, "What an astonishingly pretty girl I saw you driving with that time."

"What time?"

"I was with Lord Cleveland and we passed. You were driving your high-perch phaeton and I could not help thinking how very brave she was, as well as pretty."

"Oh—that girl. Yes, very pretty."

"I must say you have an excellent eye for pretty girls. Whenever I have seen you with a young lady, she has been excessively pretty. Are you still friends with that young lady?"

"Though it is really none of your concern, Dilys, the answer is no."

"Oh, dear me, what a set-down. And well-deserved. I do beg your pardon, cousin, for being so unconscionably nosy, but I am naturally interested about you. Why, she might have become my relative by marriage, for all I could know."

"Please try not to be such an idiot," he said coldly, and

she subsided, for his brows had drawn together forbiddingly. She was aware that she had been naughty to speak on such a subject, even though he was her cousin, but she could not forget that very beautiful creature, nor prevent herself from wondering if he still saw her, like one who cannot stop poking at an aching tooth with one's tongue. Oh, how could he help being in love with such a girl as that? Her heart was sore with the certainty that he surely must be.

Travis disapproved of Dilys' questions not only for their impropriety, but also because he knew very well she was dissembling and knew exactly what sort of girl it was who would drive about with a man unattended. Despite his displeasure, however, he felt some small bit of gratification, for it seemed to him there was an intensity behind her probing that went beyond her usual cool, almost distancing jocular manner with him.

He had found this manner disturbing, for he had known the day he came to ask her if she had refused Lord Cleveland that the impossible had happened: he had fallen in love with her. He had begun to suspect that it might be so while he was seeing Elizabeth Hayes and finding himself unable to even pretend an interest in making love to her. He knew for certain when his friend Burton had told him that Dilys had refused Lord Cleveland. At that moment he had recognized that his detestation of that gentleman was pure jealousy.

He had hoped that since he now knew his heart, he could slowly woo her to love him, but she did not seem to respond in the way he thought a girl would do when she realized a man was interested in her. She never flirted with him, or showed any awareness that his attentions were other than cousinly. Of course, he did not flirt with her either, really, or make pretty speeches or flowery compliments. He had never done so with any woman and felt only contempt for those who did, but he was beginning to feel that he must learn some new way of making a young gentlewoman aware of his feelings. He had never had experience in the art, not having had much to do with gentlewomen, young or otherwise, since the days of his foolishness with Georgeanne, and he had never paid her compliments or flirted with her. His attitude then had been a stubborn resistance to the idea of giving up what he had always considered his. It had never felt like love, or at least not as he felt now about Dilys, an emotion that sometimes, in private, he allowed to nearly swamp him with the tenderness he felt for her until his throat would tighten with tears. He simply felt the need to surround her with his love, to protect and care for her, to guard her from pain for the rest of her life.

He decided that from now on he would try to treat her more gently, to let her see something more explicit in his feelings. If then she could not accept him as a lover, he would know it at once, for it seemed to him that she was as open and clear as a sunny day, and when she looked at you with her great gray eyes, you saw only the exact truth there. It would never have occurred to him that she was capable of hiding anything from him.

The next morning he called at Brinton House, filled with his new resolution, but he found Georgeanne's drawing room swarming with young men. He was scarcely able to exchange greetings with Dilys, much less have any private words with her, and he retired from the field almost at once. That evening, however, there was another ball, and he would have an opportunity then.

He arrived earlier than was his usual wont and went straight to Georgeanne. Dilys was just being led onto the floor, and she smiled at him over her shoulder. On an impulse he asked Georgeanne to stand up with him. She enacted a farcical astonishment, then pretended to be so overcome by the honor she was close to swooning, then she accepted. They had not danced together since Georgeanne's come-out. In fact, Georgeanne had not danced often this Season—and usually only with Harry, if he came in, since she took her duties as chaperon seriously and thought, besides, that now it was Dilys' turn to shine. She also felt that a married lady with four children should refrain from causing undue gossip by showing everyone how much she enjoyed dancing.

As she and Travis passed Dilys and her partner, Dilys' eyes went wide with amazement and then she flashed them an impish grin before she was whirled away.

"I hope you are taking proper pride in your cousin's success," Georgeanne said.

"Are all these young bucks pestering her with their attentions and proposals?"

"Oh, I do not think any girl is bothered by popularity, Travis."

"Only look at that green sprig dancing with her now. Coleton's whelp, isn't it? Scarcely out of leading strings, a second son, and cares for nothing but horses, I've been told, and he dares to come sniffing around Dilys as though he had something to offer."

"You need not worry about him, Travis. I doubt she will remember his name at the end of the evening."

"Worry? Why should I worry?"

"Why, indeed?" she asked with an enigmatic smile.

He frowned and changed the subject. He returned her to her chaperon's sofa at the end of the dance and remained with her through the next set until it was time for his requested set with Dilys.

When they finally stood up together, he saw that the radiance so evident in her face before had now been replaced by a distracted air.

"Are you tired, Dilys?"

"What?"

"I asked if you were tired," he repeated patiently, biting back a more snappish retort he felt like giving her.

"Oh. No, no. I am never tired of dancing."

"I think perhaps I should not be either, if I danced always with such a light-footed partner as you," he ventured in his resolve to make her some compliments. She did not respond and he thought she had not heard him. "Dilys!"

She started. "Oh, I beg your pardon. What did you say?"

"Never mind," he said haughtily, and kept silent for some time. She looked so strange, however, that he relented at last to ask, "Dilys, what is the matter?"

"Oh, nothing. What could be wrong? Is not the music divine tonight?"

He snorted in exasperation, his new resolve breaking down in the face of such massive indifference. When the set was ended, he led her back to Georgeanne, his face stony. He bowed and asked her to forgive him but he had just remembered an appointment and could not stay for their second set.

"Oh, Travis, I am sorry. I . . ." faltered Dilys, aware that she had offended him.

"Not at all," he said with a stiff bow. "Good night, ladies," he said, and was gone.

"Oh, dear," Georgeanne said, "now what has got into him, I wonder?"

"I don't know," replied Dilys, shamefaced by this small falsehood. She knew very well he was infuriated by her inattention. She wished she had heard what he had said, for she had the impression it was something nice, but she could not bring the words into her mind no matter how hard she strained after them. Her mind, as he had spoken, had been too far away.

It had happened that just before their set, as she danced,

her ear had been caught by the name "Gallant." Instantly alert, she then heard the young lady dancing next to her continue, "Oh, I am positive of it. The author has him to the life."

"What is it called?" asked her partner.

"Well, I cannot just quite recall. Something about a rake, I know. My mama got it at Hatchard's yesterday, and I was so absolutely riveted I spent the entire day reading it." They danced away and Dilys could hear no more, but she knew they were discussing her book. It was out! She was suddenly possessed with a wild desire to see it, to actually see her words set in print. She had forgotten all about the book all these weeks, forgotten even to wonder when it would come out, and now here it was. And the girl had enjoyed it, been "riveted," she had said.

Then another thing struck her as she was led onto the floor by Travis. The first person so far as she was aware to have read the book had recognized Travis as the hero at once. "To the life," the girl had said. Oh, dear heaven, could it be so clear? Would everyone see it at once? Would Travis himself? No, surely he would never read such a book, and even if he did, he would not recognize himself. Perhaps never saw themselves as others did. But in any case, he would never read it. She was sure he was not the sort of man to read novels.

For the remainder of the evening she could not stop an endless round of questions and answers in her mind. When she was at last in bed, they continued, but now a new question arose to trouble her. Should she confess to him? No, no, no, that would be impossible and surely unnecessary. But if he brought the matter up with her, was she not in honor bound to confess? No, he would never bring it up because he would never read it, probably never even come to hear of it. Just because that silly girl had read it did not mean that anyone else would do so.

Her last thought as she drifted into sleep was to wonder how she could acquire a copy of the book.

18

He did not call today! I fear I have mortally offended him. Oh, that my wits should have deserted me at just that moment, and all over a silly book that will probably sink into oblivion without a trace! It was the praise that did it. Writers are so hungry for praise, and it was the first I have had. Mlle never praised it. Well, I must console myself that if no one else ever reads it, I have at least interested one reader. She was riveted, she said, and spent the entire day reading it. Goodness! I know I am but a poor foolish creature to be so elated by the words of such a critic, but I cannot prevent a little swelling of pride each time I remember them. I shall write Mlle today and tell her of it. She is the only person I can share these feelings with.

While Dilys wrote this, Travis was still slouched beside his breakfast table in his dressing gown, though he had been up for several hours. He was not mortally offended, but his *amour propre* was somewhat dented. He had already told himself that he had allowed his pride to lead him into behaving boorishly last night and that he should go around and apologize this very morning, but he had not done so. Instead, he had sat brooding over his breakfast, allowing his pride to have its way with him, even to the extent of trying to persuade himself that he must have mistaken his feelings about the girl. Her youth and orphaned state had roused his protective instincts, and these feelings being new to him, he had confused them with love.

He knew, however, in his heart, that this was not so, even as he tried to persuade himself it was true. What he felt for her had nothing at all to do with her youth or orphaned state, and she was much too self-possessed and strong to need his protection. What he felt was a passionate need to snatch her into his arms and make love to her, a need so strong that even thinking about it caused him to groan.

At last, unable to bear thinking of it anymore, he dressed and drove to Brinton House only to be told that my lady and Miss Bryn were from home. Of course, it was by now the middle of the afternoon, the hour of receiving callers long over. Nevertheless, he cursed under his breath at the way women must always be gallivanting about as he told his coachman to take him to his club. Perhaps Burton would be back from his visit to his mother in the country.

Travis had to while away several hours at whist before Burton made his appearance, and after greetings were exchanged, it now being time for dinner, Travis took his friend home to dine, causing his cook to lose her temper for being presented at the last moment with a guest she was unprepared for. However, a respectable meal was at last set before the two gentlemen, innocently unaware of the banging of pots and slapping of scullions that had been part of its preparation. The gentlemen paid their respects to the meal and the excellent bottle of claret that accompanied it by eating heartily and in almost complete silence until the table was cleared and the port set out. Then they pushed back their chairs, happily replete, and stretched out their long legs.

"Well, my friend, how was the country?" Travis asked.

"Boring."

"Exactly. That is why I only go there in the hunting season."

"Yes, but you haven't a mother there firing off letters by the dozens wondering why you neglect her so."

"Well, so you do neglect her."

"Wouldn't do if she were sensible and lived in town. Perfectly good house here. Cannot think why she wants to live down there in that mausoleum."

"Any company to speak of?"

"With the Season in full swing? The entire county is deserted." After a comfortable silence as they sipped appreciatively at their port, Burton added, "Met your friend Cleveland down there."

"He is not my friend. Where did you meet him?"

"Out riding, just by chance. He was alone. Forgot he had a place down there. Not the family seat, you know, but a nice bit of property. Anyway, the fellow practically begged me to come home to dinner with him. Couldn't help feeling sorry for him. Upshot was—I went. Keeps a good cellar there, I must say, but the man can't hold his wine. Got all maudlin about that little cousin of yours. He said he—"

"*What*! He dared to speak of her? What did he say, the drunken swine?"

"Lord, I could barely understand most of it. Something about being disillusioned, that she was not untouched as he—"

Travis leapt to his feet, his chair crashing back onto the floor. "Not un . . . he said Dilys was—was—"

"Am I never to be allowed to finish a sentence?" asked Burton complainingly.

"I will kill him with my bare hands!"

"Oh, no need to fly into the boughs, Gallant. He did not mean what you think, as you would know if you had not interrupted me."

Travis picked up his chair and seated himself. He took a gulp of his port, refilled his glass, and pushed the bottle toward his guest. "He had no business speaking of her at all. However, I am listening. What did he mean?"

"Well, the best I could make out, he had thought she was the embodiment of innocence. Not just never been kissed, but never even thought of love. Imagine that! M'sister never talked of anything else after she was fourteen. Always in love with someone new every week or so till the day she was married."

"I doubt Dilys has ever been in love."

"Now you're thinking just like him. That is just what he thought, what made him fall in love. Good Lord, Gallant, for a man with your reputation with the women, I would have expected you to know better than that."

"I did not have the advantage of a sister, as did you," Travis retorted, stung.

Burton laughed. "Maybe that's it, old fellow. Well, anyway, it seems Cleveland was in love with the idea of that—her never having been touched by love, I mean. Ask me, he was more in love with that idea than he was with her. I tell you the man is something short in his upper story. Sitting down there in the country alone, drinking too much most likely, and all because when he proposed, she told him she wouldn't have him because she was in love with someone else and had been since she was a child. She said she—"

Again Travis was on his feet, his chair crashed to the floor. "What! She said what?"

"There you go again. What's got into you, Gallant? Always thought you were a quiet sort of fellow. I shall get the headache if you go on throwing your chair about like that."

"Do you think he was making that up—about her being in love with someone else?"

"Oh, no. Why else would he be behaving in such a way if it wasn't true that she said it? Look here, I must be going."

"But it is early yet."

"No. Late for me. I must go home and change. Promised m'sister I would drop in on her party."

"Good heavens. What made you do that? You never go to parties."

Burton shrugged gloomily. "Sisters! Mothers! Women! They somehow make you do these things."

After he was gone Travis went to his library and threw himself down before the fire. Who could it be? Her music teacher? Some sprig met while she lived with her brother? Some married man met when she was twelve and conceived an undying passion for? He sat wrestling with the questions for hours and finally dragged himself to bed, where he slept but little. He was up at dawn, still worrying away at the problem, unable to think of what to do about it—if there was a problem—if there was anything he could do about it in any case.

His first impulse was simply to ask her outright, since he disliked any roundaboutness in his dealings with people. After some thought, however, he began to back away from the idea. He knew it was cowardly, but he feared she might take great offense at the question and repulse him completely. After Burton's remark the evening before, he was beginning to lose his confidence in his understanding of women. It was true, as Burton had said, that Travis had had a great deal of experience, and not all of them just beautiful bits of muslin. There had been any number of contessas and marchessas on the continent quite as eager as he for a discreet affair, but those women, once safely married, took affairs as a matter of course. English women of quality were a different matter. Not that there were not English ladies of quality who indulged in affairs outside their marriages, sometimes quite openly, like the notorious Lady Caroline Lamb with Byron, but for the most part they were more rigid in their morals. Travis had never dreamed of having an affair with a married lady in England, and except for Georgeanne and his Aunt Sommers, he had only nodding acquaintance with the matrons of the *ton*. As for unmarried girls of quality, they were an almost unknown species. He had always avoided them for fear of being trapped into marriage.

He wondered if she had confided her love to anyone other then Cleveland? Georgeanne, perhaps? Yes, if she had told anyone, she would have told Georgeanne, and he had no fears about asking Georgeanne bluntly. Taking heart from this thought, he called for his carriage to be brought around and hurried up to his dressing room to change.

He found Georgeanne's drawing room buzzing, as usual, but this day he had prepared himself to be patient and await his opportunity. He watched somewhat grimly as various young men came in, made their courtesies to Georgeanne, and then went to swarm about Dilys, and as several young matrons came to pay Georgeanne their duty calls. It was over an hour before there was a lessening in the coming and going and he was able to draw Georgeanne away to the far end of the room.

"Travis, my dear, how gracious of you to come here and sit glowering at my guests all morning. Whatever is wrong to cause you to behave so? You barely acknowledged Lady Moore's greeting."

"Stupid woman. Speaks only in banalities."

"She is not a tower of intellect, I agree, but that is no excuse for being rude to her."

"Oh, to the devil with Lady Moore! I did not wait about all this time to discuss her."

"I hope I am not so slow-witted as to imagine you had. So, tell me, what it is that you came to discuss."

"I suppose Dilys, ah, confides everything to you?"

"How can one know such a thing? We are very close, but even so—"

"Yes, of course," he interrupted impatiently. "Look here, Georgie, my friend Burton told me that Cleveland says that when Dilys refused him, she told him she would not have him because she loved someone else, and had done so since she was a child. Has she ever told you anything of this?"

Georgeanne's blue eyes turned violet. "How very ungallant of Lord Cleveland to spread word of such a very private business as a proposal of marriage. Surely such a conversation should never be shared with another person."

"I agree the man is a cur, but—"

"I am inexpressibly shocked by such conduct from Lord Cleveland and I shall write him of my displeasure this very day."

"You may set about him with a riding whip for all I care, I may do it myself if I run into him, but that is not what I—"

"You should not wait to run into him but take the matter into your hands at once. As her cousin, you should be equally as outraged as I."

"Well, of course I am, though the man was in his cups when he said it and it was only to Burton, who's close as a clam. He only told me because of Dilys being my cousin. But the question is—"

"And I suppose you have no fear that the next time he is flown with wine he will not give way to the same impulse?"

"Not after he gets your letter," Travis said with a grin. "Probably leave the country altogether rather than chance an encounter with you."

"He may well fear it," Georgeanne said grimly.

"Now, look here, Georgie, that is not what interests me. I want to know who it is?"

"Who it is?" Georgeanne looked blank.

"The man! The one she's been in love with for so long. Surely she has confided it to you?"

"And if she had, do you think I would break her confidence by telling you?"

He stared at her for a long moment, his brows drawn together. At last he said grudgingly, "No, I suppose you could not. Oh, devil take it!"

She looked at him commiseratingly. She knew very well what was his trouble, and could have told him what she guessed to be the state of Dilys' heart, but she despised people who interfered in intimate matters. She felt such things were best left to be worked out between the people involved, and though she could have made things easier for him, she would not do so. Besides, it would do no harm for things to be difficult for Travis, who had had his way made too easy for him with his title and money and good looks.

"Travis, my dear," she said kindly, "Dilys has never told me of any secret love. Perhaps she only said it to put Lord Cleveland off. In my opinion, he was overly confident of his conquest and in such cases gentlemen can be difficult to dissuade."

He brightened. "Yes. I suppose it could be so."

"Will you be attending the Waughs' dinner this evening?"

"Will I see you there—and Dilys?"

"Oh, indeed," she said with a laugh. "Now, if you want to speak to her, you'd best do so, for she and I have an appointment with the dressmaker in half an hour."

Travis bowed and made his way down the room, pushed his way through the crowd to Dilys' side, and in low voice told her he had come to apologize for his behavior the previous evening. She smiled up at him dazzlingly, her heart much relieved, and said she had understood completely if he had become irritated with her when she was being so absentminded and inattentive. She hoped very much that he would repeat whatever it was that he had said, but he only bent to kiss her hand and said he would see her at the Waughs' later and went away.

She was content, however.

19

He apologized to me this morning for cutting our second set. I was so astonished, but, oh, so glad. I wish we could have had more time to speak, but there were so many callers today. It was odd, for he stayed quite a time, sitting apart and looking so forbidding, then he took Georgie to the other end of the room and they talked for some time together. I could hear nothing of what they said, of course, but it seemed to me Georgie was angry about something for a time, though they parted friends, I could see. When I asked her if he had upset her, she laughed and said, Certainly not. Oh, well, I will see him again tonight.

When Dilys, with Georgeanne and Harry, arrived in the Waughs' drawing room, where only half the company was assembled, three ladies on a sofa were informing several others of the new book they had read, so the first words Dilys heard as she entered the room were, ". . . but, my dear, you simply must read it. *The Story of a Rake* it is called."

"And you will have no trouble recognizing the hero. It is Lord Travis Gallant."

"Good heavens! I must get it at once."

Dilys shrank back behind Georgeanne. How dreadful! More people were reading the book and identifying Travis—and he would soon be here. Would they go on speaking of it before his face?

After greetings, the ladies lost no time in acquainting Georgeanne and Dilys of the latest *on-dit.* Georgeanne was amused, but disbelieving at first. However, the ladies persisted in claiming Travis as the model for the hero and at last her eyes darkened with displeasure.

"I feel sure my cousin Travis," she said coolly, only slightly underlining the relationship, "will be most amused to think you see him as the hero of a novel. I have heard that Mrs. Gore-Trillin has become so ill she was forced to retire to the country. Can this be true?"

The excited females took the hint and spoke of it to Georgeanne no more, and after that, the passing on of this bit of gossip to newly arrived guests was carried on in whispers, but it was definitely carried on. When Travis came in—the last to arrive, as usual—every eye in the room swiveled in his direction and all talk ceased for a moment. He seemed not to notice, and after greeting his host and hostess, he came directly to Dilys, who was standing with Georgeanne and Harry. He bowed, kissed Georgeanne's hand, then Dilys', and shook hands with Harry, who clapped him on the shoulder in the most friendly manner. Travis looked startled but pleased. Harry had also heard the gossip and resented it. He immediately began a lively conversation with Travis about the spavined nag old Chamfers had been persuaded to buy. The four of them presented a warmly united family front to the rest of the room.

When dinner was announced, Travis found he had been given Dilys to take in to dinner, since Lady Waugh had begun to suspect his partiality for the girl. She had a warm spot in her heart for Travis and wanted to make him happy at her dinner party.

He was so, and devoted the evening to Dilys with a single-mindedness that caused almost as much talk and significantly raised eyebrows as *The Story of a Rake.* In fact, these two items were very nearly all that was talked of that evening.

Travis heard none of it. He was telling Dilys about his boyhood, his young manhood, and about the waste he felt his life to have been until now. He ignored the lady on his left completely, but she only shrugged and smiled and waited uncomplainingly for her own dinner partner to be finished with the lady on his other side. After all, young love, said her amused glance around the table.

Dilys, her heart bumping about almost painfully in her breast, listened and sympathized and wondered. Most of all wondered. And then, most surprising of all, when he bid her good night, he asked if he might see her alone the following morning. She said yes without even applying to Georgeanne for permission. She was sure Georgeanne would not object. Alone! He wanted to see her alone! She could not prevent herself from imagining that it might be to make a declaration, though she tried to tell herself it could not be so.

Georgeanne, when belatedly informed of his request, felt her own heart leap with happiness. However, she only said quite calmly that since it was not one of her days for receiving callers, there would be no problem, but she suggested that Dilys meet him in the back drawing room just in case. "And I hope it will not be for more than a half-hour, darling, for proprieties' sake. You know I am not a great stickler for all that business of not trusting two people to be alone together, but it won't do to give the servants too much to gossip about."

The back drawing room was used mostly by Georgeanne and Harry for romps with their children every day for an hour or so before the children's supper. It was always cluttered with toys and games, unless there was a large evening party, when it was cleared and opened up into the series of three ground-floor reception rooms. Dilys went down early and wandered about, picking up toys and putting them down. When the door opened to admit Travis, she was holding a jack-in-the box that popped up the instant he entered.

She said, ''Oh,'' and laughed a little breathlessly.

Travis smiled and closed the door and came up to her. After much thought he had decided that he must ask her his question even though he lost her, for there could be no peace for him until he knew.

''Dilys, forgive me, but I must ask you something that may not please you.''

She turned a little pale. So it was not what she had thought. She had been a fool again. ''Yes,'' she said, raising her chin bravely.

''I have heard that you told Cleveland you could not marry him because you had been in love since childhood with someone. I must know if this is true.''

She stared for a moment and then looked away, a blush restoring some of her color. ''He should not have repeated our conversation.''

''I agree. Who is it, Dilys?''

''I cannot think by what right you come here and interrogate me!''

''That is two questions you have not answered.'' With his finger he turned her face back to his own. ''Is it true, Dilys?''

At last she raised her eyes to his and looked straight at him, and he knew before her simple ''Yes'' that is was indeed true. He was shaken and realized that until that moment he had been sure it was not so, only something to rid herself of Cleveland's importunities, as Georgeanne had suggested.

''Who is it? No, do not turn away from me again. I must know.''

''Why must you know?''

''Because I must! I . . . Dilys . . .'' He faltered to a halt and dropped his hand from her face. A long silence ensued.

At last he said, his voice hoarse, "I must know if—if he is worthy of you."

She stared at him in surprise. He had never spoken to her in such a way before. He was always rather terse and sure of himself. She wanted to put her arms around him and comfort him, for he seemed so unhappy. Suddenly she said, "Wait here. I will only be one moment," and ran out of the room.

He was still staring at the door when she returned, panting, and held out to him on her hand a square of white linen. He took it, looked at it and then back at her, bewildered.

"What is it?"

"It is a handkerchief. See." She turned it over and there in the corner was embroidered the initial G.

"Who—who does this belong to?"

"It belongs to you. That is your initial."

"I don't understand. Where did you find it?"

"I did not find it. You gave it to me."

"I?"

"Yes. When I was nine. You came to visit me at Alun's after my parents were drowned, and when I cried, you gave me your handkerchief."

"And you kept it all this time?"

"Yes. It was very bad of me not to return it, I suppose."

"Why did you keep it?"

"I needed it," she said simply, her gray eyes looking into his, and he saw there everything he wanted to see, all he wanted to know.

"Dilys, my darling girl, will you marry me?"

"Oh, yes!"

And then at last he had her close in his arms and was kissing her as he had imagined doing so often. She, being as eager as he, it was quite some time before they could be satisfied. At last they drew back and looked dazedly into each other's eyes.

"I was the one, then, whom you loved since you were a child?"

"Since the day you allowed me to cry into your neckcloth and ruin it."

"Why did you never tell me or—or—"

"How could I even dream that you would want to hear?"

After that there were a great many misunderstandings to clear up and questions to be answered and reassurances to be given, as well as such important matters as when the other first "knew," interspersed with further demonstrations of love.

Meanwhile, Georgeanne had been called from her boudoir, where she was spending the time trying to be patient as she waited for the outcome of the meeting in the back drawing room. It seemed that Lady Sommers had called to see her. She felt a flash of irritation in the inopportunity of the visit, but shook it off and hurried downstairs. She was very fond of Aunt Sommers, in reality her great-aunt, being her grandfather Langthorne's sister.

Lady Sommers raised her cheek for Georgeanne's kiss and complimented her upon her looks, and then came straight to the point. "Is Travis going to make an offer for Dilys?"

Georgeanne gasped in astonishment, then burst out laughing. "My goodness, how can you have heard that?"

"My dear, I know everyone worth knowing in this town— indeed in England. I had a note with my breakfast chocolate from a guest of Lady Waugh's dinner party last night to tell me that in her opinion a declaration was imminent."

"Dear heaven! Well, then, they are in the back drawing room at this moment, and I believe, I hope, that is the purpose of his visit."

"Lady Bryn," announced the butler from the door, and Caroline marched in. Georgeanne's heart sank.

"Georgeanne, what is this I hear?" Caroline began demandingly.

"Good morning, Caroline. You are aquainted with my aunt, Lady Sommers?"

Caroline looked annoyed when she saw the old lady, but dipped her a curtsy and sat down. "Well, since we are all family, I will not mince my words."

"I am sure you would never do that," Georgeanne murmured.

"I do not believe in beating about the bush. It is a waste of time. Now, it has just come to my ears that Travis Gallant is making a deliberate push to attach Dilys' affections and a proposal is expected at any moment. Is this true?"

"Heaven help us," Georgeanne cried. "May I ask where you have heard of this?"

"A friend of mine has an acquaintance who was a guest at Lady Waugh's last night and saw them there. She said they were perfectly disgraceful, practically making love before the entire table."

"That is untrue, and you must know it, for your friend could not have failed to mention that Harry and I were also present. You cannot believe we would allow anything unseemly to go on, or that Dilys herself would behave with such a lack of decorum."

"I was told they barely spoke to anyone else," persisted Caroline stubbornly.

"They certainly had a great deal to say to each other, or at least Travis did, Dilys mostly listened. However, there was nothing unseemly about it, I assure you."

"You have not answered my question, I notice," snapped Caroline. "Has he proposed?"

"Not to my knowledge," Georgeanne hedged.

"Do you expect him to do so?"

"I believe it is a possibility."

"And you can sit there and tell me this with such complacency?"

"Well, you asked me, Caroline," said Georgeanne mildly.

"But you cannot approve!"

"Oh, but I can."

"For that matter, so do I," put in Lady Sommers stoutly.

"No, no, no! It will never do! The man is an out-and-out dissolute, degenerate rake!"

"How dare you—" began Geogeanne angrily.

"But they do say," broke in Lady Sommers, who was enjoying herself hugely, "that the worst rakes make the best husbands. Sowed their wildest oats in advance, don't you see?"

"I do not see! No decent woman will have him in her drawing room, and you approve of him as a husband for—"

"Dear me, Lady Bryn," said Lady Sommers, "you are sadly out of touch with reality. There may be a few old-fashioned sticklers who would not have him, but you may take my word for it that most of the *ton* are delighted when he accepts their invitations. Unless you consider them all indecent women, like dear Lady Waugh last night."

"That is neither here nor there; the question is about his pursuit of Dilys. I think it is outrageous of you to even contemplate such a marriage, and I tell you now it will never be allowed. Alun will never give his permission for such an alliance," stormed Caroline.

"I do not think we will need to trouble Alun for his permission," Georgeanne said in a steely voice.

"Of course they must have his permission! She is only seventeen years old. She cannot marry him without Alun's permission. Certainly not before she is one-and-twenty, and I cannot see Travis Gallant waiting about for four years," replied Caroline triumphantly.

"He will not need to do so. He will have my permission."

"You have nothing to say to it."

"Oh, but I have everything to say to it. I am Dilys' sole guardian, according to my father's will. After me, Harry, and if both of us are deceased before she comes of age, my father's solicitor. Alun does not come into it at all. My father had the right to make that decision because Dilys was legally adopted by him before she was three weeks old.''

This was such a telling blow that Caroline was still opening and closing her mouth wordlessly, her face nearly purple, and old Lady Sommers was still applauding softly when the door opened and Travis and Dilys entered, hand in hand, their faces glowing with such happiness that the story was told without the need for words.

Lady Sommers rose and held out her arms to Travis and he went to her and completely enveloped her tiny frame in a bear hug. ''My boy, my dear, dear boy. I knew you would come in a winner at last,'' she cried, the tears running unheeded down her wrinkled old face.

Georgeanne went to Dilys and kissed her fervently. Then Travis released Lady Sommers and came to Georgeanne and she kissed him also. ''I see you know already,'' he said.

''I know—and I had hoped very much,'' she said happily.

''Well, it is true. I suppose I must apply to someone for permission. Harry? Or—''

''No, only to me, and my permission is hereby given.''

''Well, I do not approve and never shall,'' cried Caroline, rising angrily.

They all started in surprise, having forgotten all about Caroline. ''Oh, Caroline—I did not see you. Surely you will wish me happy,'' Dilys said coaxingly, in her happiness wanting even Caroline to smile.

''Never! Never, do you hear? I will never receive a Lady Gallant in my drawing room, not even if it is you.'' With that Caroline stormed out of the room.

They all stared after her in shock until Travis said in such astonishment they all burst out laughing, ''She seems to think a Lady Gallant would want to be received by her.''

20

I am in such a daze most of the time that I sometimes forget to write down my thoughts, and yet now it is only by writing down each day's events and conversations that they become real to me and not some daydream of what would make me most happy in the world. Oh, the heaven of being loved by him. How could I ever have thought him arrogant, or have been a little frightened by him? He is so kind, so gentle with me, and yet he is the reverse of overblown complimentary speeches. He says he is not good at that drawing-room dandy behavior, and he is not! But his eyes are so soft when he looks at me, they seem to say everything.

The book is very much the talk of the *ton* and I worry that he may hear of it from some gossip eager to twit him about it, but so far he seems oblivious. I do so wish I had never written it, nor allowed it to see print. I can only pray the furor will die down soon.

The day Dilys wrote the above, Georgeanne came home with a newly purchased copy of *The Story of a Rake*, and sat up late into the night to finish reading it.

"Well, Dilly," she said over breakfast the next morning, "it is certainly a book that is difficult to put down, if only because one dreads, or perhaps hopes, to find oneself portrayed in it."

"And did you?" Dilys asked cautiously.

"Lord, no, but I think I recognized nearly everyone else in it, and there can be no doubt Travis was the model for the hero."

"Oh, dear," was all Dilys could think of in reply.

"It is no doubt written by one of the many young ladies who have been infatuated with him."

"Why do you think so," Dilys asked breathlessly.

"Well, it is a loving portrait, despite the wickedness of the man's ways. He is not depicted as evil, you see, only a man driven to excesses by his frustration in an early love affair. He is never mean or vicious, and does a great many kindnesses for his friends and those in need. In fact, very like Travis."

"I m-m-must read it," Dilys stuttered, flustered by having to speak what amounted to a falsehood by implications to her own dear sister.

"Of course you must, or you will not be able to carry on an intelligent conversation for weeks, since that is all anyone is talking about. I have finally had to give up my tactics of bestowing a frozen stare on anyone who dares say it is about Travis, or I should have no friends left at all. And anyway now that I have read it, I must say that I agree that it is."

"I do hope some new thing happens to make everyone forget all about it—for Travis' sake. Do you think he will get to hear of it?"

"I cannot think of anyone hwo would have the nerve to actually bring up the subject to him," Georgeanne said with a laugh. Then her eyes kindled with mischief, "Except Caroline. With her lack of tact she might—if she were on speaking terms with him."

Dilys shuddered at the thought, but then remembered. "No fear. Caroline never read a book in all the time I lived in her house. She thinks reading is a waste of time."

This was true of Caroline, but though she couldn't be

bothered to read, she had heard all about the book—through her usual source of all knowledge, gossip—not long after her attack against Travis in Georgeanne's drawing room. It was gossip, in fact, that took up so much of the time she claimed reading books wasted, for she did little else. She carried a workbasket about with her, and at times even took some embroidery from it, but it was only for the look of it, for she seldom set a stich in the slightly grubby scarf she invariably pulled forth. She rarely saw her children unless they were fetched, rosy and damp from their baths, to be cooed over by her dinner guests, or if they had a new piece to recite and were brought down to do so for the delection of morning callers. True, she had a half-hour session with her housekeeper every morning to go over menus or to arrange for a party. Other than that, however, she did little else but receive and pay calls, give and attend dinners and occasional parties, and drive in the park. Apart, that is, from meddle.

The fact is, Caroline had only two interests in life: money and meddling. Money was for accumulating, for she was notoriously closefisted, and the accumulation had become almost a sickness as she had matured. As a child and young girl, her family had been always scrimping and doing without, especially after their precarious rise to squirehood, when the need to keep up appearances had caused them to spend more than they could really afford. Her mother, being a vicar's daughter, had never let anyone forget her superior social status and had fostered in her daughter a snobbishness that had also grown with the years.

After a lucky investment paid off, her father had reinvested in the importing of cocoa and made a fortune and was eventually given his title after making a substantial contribution to the queen's favorite charity. This had made possible an elaborate come-out for Caroline and the acquiring of Alun as a husband. Her mother had hoped for an earl, at least, but as Caroline's only offer, after three Seasons, was from Alun, she had had to be content.

Possibly Caroline would have been a meddler if she had remained in the lower branches of the squirarchy, but money and a title had certainly given her more scope, and she did not hesitate to attempt to order the managements of her friends' lives. She was insatiable for the smallest details of those lives, since one could never know what might come in handy when trying to manipulate others to her own desires.

Not being well-liked by the cream of the *ton*, those people who were close to Georgeanne and Harry, her cronies quite often came to her with gossip that was not the latest of news. Thus she had been just too late to interfere in Dilys' refusal of Lord Cleveland and in her acceptance of Travis.

It was four days after Dilys heard the first hint of her book being read by a member of the public before Caroline was brought news of it. The friend who carried the gossip to her had only just heard of it and had not had time to read the book herself. Caroline all but ordered the woman to buy the book that very day, read it, and report back the next day. The lady made a feeble protest, but overcome by Caroline's more powerful personality, she at last agreed.

When she obediently returned on the following day, her eyes still bloodshot with the task assigned her, the book only half-finished, she was grateful to find another caller with Caroline who had read the entire book. Between them they were able to give Caroline a very full report on the book, naming all the characters and indentifying all of them with their real-life models, old Ottway, Lady Belnord, and the Harrison sisters, as well as Travis, and the full details of his life of dissolution.

Caroline had not thought what she might do with all this information, or even why she was so interested, since it was now too late to use it to interfere between Travis and Dilys. However, she was still smarting from her complete rout by Georgeanne in the matter, and so she went blindly on, collecting information about the book, hoping for something she could use against Georgeanne.

Her patience was at last rewarded, she thought, when her friend the Hon. Mrs. Johnstrow told her that a friend, Lady Hall, had a daughter at school with a certain Miss Threese, who claimed to have discovered the manuscript of *The Story of a Rake*, and to have been responsible for its being published.

"Pho, pho, all self-aggrandizment! How could she have been responsible, a mere schoolgirl? Where could she have got the manuscript."

"From her governess, it seems, who received it from a former pupil, and she read it on the sly—the girl, I mean, and was so taken with it she showed it to her parents and they—"

"Who is this governess?" Caroline asked, feeling a tingling of excitement.

"Well, I do not recall that her name was mentioned."

"But that is the most important part! We must know who is this governess."

"But whatever for?" asked the astounded Mrs. Johnstrow.

"Because it will lead to the writer, of course. Really, I should have thought that was obvious," Caroline added witheringly. "If we know the governess, we will find the former pupil."

"Well, it would be great fun to know, before everyone else, who wrote the book," said Mrs. Johnstrow, catching the excitement. "I mean, that is what everyone is teasing themselves about now that they have picked the bones of the characters and identified them all."

"Then go back to Lady Hall and find out the governess's

name as soon as possible, and perhaps you shall be the first to know,'' Caroline said, though naturally she had no intention of allowing such a stunning morsel of gossip as that to be disseminated by anyone other than herself.

It was several days before Mrs. Johnstrow managed to find out the name of the governess, and she hurried at once to Caroline with her news. When she pronounced the name, Caroline felt every nerve end in her body jump as from a jolt of electricity.

''Ah,'' she said on a great sigh of pleasure, ''Mademoiselle Fleury. Now we may learn something interesting.''

But in truth she already knew it all and had not the least qualm of conscience in withholding her knowledge from her friend. For she had seen in a flash of a second that Georgeanne must be the authoress of the book. She had been Mademoiselle Fleury's pupil from her sixth year until her come-out. Caroline could remember the woman clearly and calculated she could not be more than five-and-thirty now, which meant that she was no more than eighteen when she began with Georgeanne and could surely have had no other pupil before that. So only Georgeanne and this Threese girl, and of course Dilys, had been her pupils, but Dilys had been but nine when she left Mademoiselle Fleury, and Caroline dismissed the idea of Dilys without further thought. She was much too gleeful with the idea of Georgeanne being the culprit to want it to be anyone else. What, she wondered, would the high and mighty Lord Travis feel about that treachery?

When Mrs. Johnstrow had taken her leave, Caroline felt so burdened with her budget of news that she felt compelled to leave her house. She must tell someone or burst. She called for her carriage and had herself driven to the park. She would be sure to meet there someone worthy upon whom to bestow this titillating *on-dit*.

She let several imposing matrons go by, all worthy, but she would decide after she had seen everyone who was out today. There might be someone better. Then she saw the young Duchess of Portshire driving toward her, and her heart bounded up in her chest with joy. She had met the duchess once, but had not succeeded in obtaining more from her than a nod and a smile. She had sent cards to the duchess for her grandest parties, but had only received that lady's regrets. She had never received a card to one of the duchess's entertainments. Now she felt she had the key to open those doors, for the duchess could not help but be gratified to receive this confidence before anyone else in town. Caroline felt so emboldened that she did not hesitate to order her driver to pull up, all the while waving her hand wildly at the other carriage.

"Who on earth is that strange creature waving at you, Hermione?" drawled her brother, seated beside her in the carriage.

"I do not know, dear, but she clearly means us to stop. Pull up, Chumb," the duchess ordered. She was a most amiable young woman.

"Duchess, how lovely to see you today, and how charming you are looking," gushed Caroline.

"Thank you. Ah, have you met my brother, Lord Burton—Lady, er?"

Even to Caroline it was clear the duchess had no idea who she was, but she was not in the least abashed. "Lady Bryn, Duchess, we met at Lady White's charity musicale. Happy to make your acquaintance, Lord Burton."

Lord Burton bowed, his sister smiled good-naturedly, and they both waited. When nothing more seemed forthcoming, the duchess said, "Lovely day, is it not? So nice to have seen you, Lady Bryn," and turned to order her coachman to drive on.

In a panic that she might lose her audience, Caroline blurted out, "Oh, you must not go, dear Duchess, I must tell you. I mean, have you read that book everyone is talking of? The one about the rake, I mean."

"I have heard the talk, but not read it myself as yet."

"Oh, it is scandalous, really. All about that dreadful Lord Travis Gallant and his decadent ways."

The duchess stiffened. "He is a very good friend of my family, madam."

"Well, er, I mean—of course, it is only a story, and I form my opinion by what is written in the book, not being personally acqainted with the gentleman."

"Engaged to your sister, isn't he?" barked Burton, who had realized who this odious woman must be.

"That was done against my advice," Caroline blurted out before she could stop herself; then, recovering quickly, she continued, "I objected, you see, because I knew him so little, and—and thought she was already betrothed to Lord Cleveland, a charming gentleman," she finished happily, feeling she had redeemed herself.

"Well, I will wish you good day, Lady—" began the duchess coldly.

"Oh, but I have not told you. You see, I have discovered who is the authoress of the book and have not breathed a word to another soul. So you will be first among all your friends with the news!" That should fetch her, Caroline thought, but the duchess only stared at her, horror-struck, though to Caroline she seemed wide-eyed with anticipation. "It is Georgeanne Brinton," she announced triumphantly, her voice rising shrilly with excitement.

"Drive on, Chumb. Good day to you, Lady Bryn," said the duchess, and was driven away.

Burton glanced at his sister. Her face stiff and pale with indignation. "Not to take it all so to heart, my dear. Only a social climber trying to ingratiate herself with you. She is a poisonous woman. Gallant has told me of her.''

"Vulgar, underbred creature! I cannot bear such gossip.''

"Well, my dear, and neither can I. I wonder if you would mind dropping me off at my club. I think I had better speak to Brinton about this matter.''

"Surely you will not pass it on,'' protested his sister.

"Only to Brinton. Someone has to stop that woman's mouth, and I think Georgeanne's husband the proper person to deal with it.''

Caroline watched indignantly as they were driven away. Stiff-necked prigs, she fumed, to behave in such a way to me and at the same time claim Travis Gallant as a friend! Probably no better than he is under that facade. I wish I had not told her, after all. I should have saved it for someone more appreciative. After a time, however, her temper cooled, and because she could not quite make herself truly angry with a duchess, she began to tell herself that she had mistaken the duchess's attitude. Was it not just as possible that she had only pretended to be offended because her brother was there and she did not like him to think she was interested in gossip. No doubt her abrupt departure was caused only by her eagerness to pass along the gossip to her friends. Yes, yes, it must be so!

Caroline settled back against the squabs with a sigh of relief at this interpretation of events. She thought, Perhaps in a few days, even possibly a week or so, the duchess will remember that she owes me a favor and send me a card for a party. Caroline's thoughts drifted off blissfully to the time when she could begin a conversation with "As the dear duchess—that's the Duchess of Portshire, you know—said to me only last night at dinner . . .''

21

Our announcement of betrothal appeared in the papers today. Georgeanne and I went to consult with Madame Graumont about my wedding dress. The veil will be Mama's lace from her own wedding, which Georgeanne also wore for hers. We have asked ten young ladies to attend me who have become friends during this Season. I wanted only Georgeanne, but she says I must have a bevy of maidens; she intends to stand in as mother-of-the-bride. Harry is to give me away. We very properly asked Alun to do this, but Alun declined! Georgeanne says no doubt Caroline refused to allow him to participate. When we returned from Madame Graumont's there were fourteen calling cards left at the door.

This entry was written on the same day that Caroline had accosted the Duchess of Portshire and Lord Burton, and Burton wasted little time in seeking out Harry at his club.

"A word with you, Brinton, and it please you."

"With pleasure, sir," said Harry, excusing himself from the group who stood with him.

Burton drew him away into an empty side room. "I have just come from a drive with m'sister. We were stopped by that Bryn woman. Relative of your wife, isn't she?"

"Oh, yes, Alun's wife. He is Dilys' brother."

"That's the one. Odious woman."

"She is unpleasant, to be sure," Harry said with a laugh.

"Dammed unpleasant this morning, I can assure you. Suppose you know about this book that's all the talk now?"

"Yes, I've heard about it. Couldn't avoid it, really. Supposed to be modeled on Gallant, they say."

"Damn-fool nonsense, the whole business!"

"Oh, well, they must have something to put their heads together about. I daresay some new scandal will come along next week and the book will be forgotten."

"Not if that Bryn woman has anything to do with it. Told my sister this morning your wife had written it."

"What? Good God, where on earth could she have heard such a thing?"

"Made it up, most likely. M'sister didn't wait to hear. Snubbed her a treat and drove away. But I thought you should know about it. The woman claimed m'sister was the first she had told it to, but the Lord knows how many others she met on her way home and blabbed it to. Don't know if there is much you can do to stop her."

Harry looked grim. "Well, I will certainly try. Thank you, Burton, for telling me of this. If you will excuse me now, I will go and find Bryn."

Harry was by nature genial and the best-natured fellow in the world, his temper slow to kindle. He hated only injustice, social climbers, and liars, but even these did not cause him to lose his temper. Only attacks against his loved ones could do that. By the time he ran Alun to earth in his club he had reached, not a boiling point, but certainly a slow smoldering. He drew Alun aside and went straight at the business.

"I must speak to you about your wife, sir."

"My wife?"

"Yes. Just an hour or so ago she met the Duchess of Portshire in the park and told her that that book about the rake was written by my wife."

"Oh, I think it is always a mistake to listen to women's tittle-tattle," said Alun with a shrug.

"Ordinarily I would agree with you. But not when it is about my family—and yours, I may add."

Alun looked about uneasily. "My dear fellow, storm in a teacup, don't you see? I should just ignore the entire business if I were you."

"If you were me you would feel very differently. I will not have anyone—*anyone*—going about making up such lies and spreading them about town when they concern my wife."

"Oh, here, now—lies? I cannot like that allegation at all, sir," said Alun pompously.

"No more than I like them being made, sir. My wife did not write that book. She could not have done so without my being aware of it."

"I think they get up to a great deal they never tell us," Alun said with a placating smile.

"Your wife may, *mine* does not! She has been in India for seven years. She has had four children and the ordering of a very large household. Apart from that, we have spent too much of that time actually in each other's company for her to have enough time left over to write a book. No, sir, it is an outright lie, and it is being put about by your wife. I think these assurances on my part must be sufficient to persuade you of the truth in this matter. If not, I shall hold you responsible."

Alun blanched. "Now, look here, Briton, I . . . This is all . . . Are you challenging me?"

"I am warning you. Look to your wife, sir! Good day."

Alun stared after Harry as he stalked away, fear startling him out of his usual complacency. Could it be possible Brinton meant to call him out? Alun broke out in a cold sweat at the thought, for he had never trained at pistols or swords. He had a great fear of any combat at all, and all his life had sedulously avoided any argument that might lead to such a thing, developing along the way a thick-skinned imperviousness to all slights and insults that came his way. He was a man who refused to lose his temper under any provocation, and here he was being put into the position of possibly being forced into a duel by some tarradiddle put about by his wife.

Caroline! Good God, what was he to do about her? He had never opposed her in their life together. It had always been too much trouble, since she always had her own way in the end.

By the time he entered his own front door, he was quaking inside, his fear of speaking to his wife almost as great as his fear of not doing so. "Where is Lady Bryn?" he asked the footman as he handed him his hat and cane.

"In the drawing room, m'lord, with Mrs. Johnstrow."

Alun felt a sense of reprieve, for he would not be able to speak to her just now if someone was with her. It was only a momentary reprieve, however, for even as he entered the room, he heard his wife saying, ". . . but of course I am right. It is definitely Georgeanne Brinton who wrote the book. It could not be anyone else. Why, Bryn, what brings you home at this time of day?"

"My dear. Mrs. Johnstrow," he bowed. "I am very much afraid that you are incorrect in your surmise, my love."

"I beg your pardon, sir?" Caroline looked at him in astonishment, as well she might, never having heard any contradictory words from him.

"I say that it cannot be true that Georgeanne wrote that book," he repeated stolidly, knowing he had gone too far to retreat now, even had he wanted to.

"I am afraid you can know little, if anything, about the matter, sir, and therefore cannot be qualified to speak," Caroline said angrily.

Mrs. Johnstrow rose hastily to her feet. "I really must go

along now—several calls to make, you know. Good day, Lord Bryn, good day, dear Caroline.'' She retreated in a great fluster that was not even noticed by the Bryns.

Caroline continued irritably. ''Really, Bryn, I do not appreciate you starting rows in my drawing room before my friends.''

''I beg your pardon, my dear, but I could not let you say that to her without interrupting. I must insist that you stop telling people that Georgeanne Brinton wrote that book.''

''Insist? You amaze me, sir!''

''Yes, no doubt, but in this you will heed me. Brinton was onto me just now. He had already heard it from Burton, who came hotfoot to tell him it was you spreading the tale. He was very angry and assured me it could not be so.''

''Well, naturally he would,'' Caroline retorted sarcastically. ''Nevertheless, it is so.''

''I do not care if it is. *You* must stop going about saying it is so,'' he replied heatedly, his fear giving him strength.

''I shall do as I like, sir!''

''Damn me if you will.''

''How dare you use such language to me?''

At last roused to real anger, he said forcefully, ''Because you do not listen to me! I will be obeyed in this. If you will not, I shall be forced to remove you to the country tomorrow.''

Now Caroline was truly dumbfounded. ''You would not dare. I cannot believe . . . Have you lost your senses entirely?'' she cried shrilly.

''No, but I might very well lose my life if you persist in this foolishness.''

''Your life? Now you are being ridiculous,'' she said scornfully.

''No, I am not. Brinton as good as told me he would call me out if you did not stop. Perhaps you will not mind if he does. Give you another damn thing to gossip about! But I shall not like it at all, I assure you. You *will* stop, and that's an end to it.''

Caroline sat down abruptly upon the sofa, for once unable to think of anything to say. Her mouth opened and closed silently several times. At last she whispered, ''Call you out?'' is disbelieving tones.

''Yes. And if I hear any breath of *that* going about, I shall know where it comes from and know what to do about it,'' he threatened grimly.

''Surely you cannot think I would tell anyone such a thing as that?''

''You were not above starting that hare about Georgeanne. Good God, Caroline, have you no shame? Georgeanne Brinton is my first cousin. Related to you by marriage. Surely you should be above slinging mud at your own family?''

She began to cry, since she could not think of anything else to do to calm his anger. It worked, for Alun had had so little experience with women that their tears made him awkward and uneasy, and even more distressing, guilty.

''Now, then—now then, no need for that, Caroline. You have made a mistake, but anyone may do that. No doubt I spoke too harshly. We will forget it all and pray the matter will go no further.''

It was too late for that, however. Mrs. Johnstrow told her husband that very evening and on the following day passed it on to several friends. Within two days the town was buzzing with the news. It never reached Georgeanne herself or Dilys, for, though her friends had heard it, they would not speak of it before her or her sister. It did reach Mlle., however, who had it from her precocious former charge, Miss Threese. Miss Threese attended an academy for young ladies now, but Mlle. remained in residence in charge of the youngest Threese daughter.

"You will never guess, Mademoiselle. All the girls at school can talk of nothing else. It seems your mysterious former pupil has been given a name at last."

"Please try to speak a little more coherently, Mademoiselle Threese," said Mlle. calmly. She always spoke to Miss Threese in calming tones since Miss Threese had a tendency to volatility.

"The one who wrote *The Story of a Rake*. Several of the girls have heard it from their mamas. I do think it is too bad that they should know before me when it was I who—"

Mlle. felt a profound dismay, though she did not allow Miss Threese to see it. "Who are they saying is the author?"

"Lady Brinton! They say she is the most beautiful lady in London and—"

"Lady Brinton did not write the book."

"But they say she was your former pupil. Oh, I do wish you had told me."

"I repeat, Mademoiselle Threese, Lady Brinton did not write the book."

"But—"

"I never dreamed there would be all this unseemly gossip, or I should never have allowed the book to be published." She sat for a moment in silence, then made up her mind what she must do. She turned to Miss Threese. "The truth of the matter is that I wrote the book myself."

Miss Threese stared at her in stupefaction, her mouth, opened to protest yet again, remained open. After a moment she said falteringly, "But, Mademoiselle, how—how could you have? You—surely you did not know Lord Travis Gallant?"

"I have known him since he was a small boy. He is Lady Brinton's cousin and they played together as children. Naturally I have been interested in his life since then."

Miss Threese was silenced—and convinced. Even apart

from this last evidence put before her, she knew that Mlle.
never, but never, told an untruth.

When she had an hour to herself later that same day, Mlle.
wrote to Mr. Conklin of Conklin, Burrows, Publishers, to
advise them that she had changed her mind about remaining
anonymous, since she had learned that an innocent person
was being accused of being the author. Since this was false,
the author's true name, Mlle. Hortense Fleury, should be
announced by the publishers to the public as soon as possible.

22

Aunt Sommers gave a dinner to introduce me to Travis' family. There are not so very many, a few aunts and cousins, besides Travis' brother, the present Duke of Trevithick. He came with his duchess and *she* is ever so intimidating. Regal as a queen, but quite nice when she knows you better. She and the duke gave me an emerald and diamond bracelet and necklace as a wedding present. I was so overcome I could barely stutter out an adequate thank-you. Travis and his brother seem to quite like each other, though they are not at all alike except in coloring. The duke is something pompous at first, but unbent a little as the evening went on. Travis was all smiles, not one forbidding glower all evening. In fact, he is more and more warm and open. I believe it is his true nature, released by happiness. Oh, I pray I shall always make him happy. My gown is finished, the final banns will be read next Sunday, and the wedding one week later.

Travis was indeed a much-changed man, as all his friends and acquaintances were astonished to see. He greeted every-one warmly and even allowed himself to be taken by the arm and addressed at length by some of his club's worst bores, a thing he had never allowed before now.

One of these gentlemen was Mr. Johnstrow, husband of Caroline's friend, who drank a great deal more than he could hold and while in his cups considered himself a great wit and raconteur. He was universally avoided during these times if it was at all possible to do so.

One evening after dining *en famille* with the Brintons and Dilys, Travis dropped into his club to say hello to Burton. Burton was not there when he arrived, but he encountered Mr. Johnstrow holding forth to a group of gentlemen who all started nervously when Travis entered the room.

Mr. Johnstrow, made bold by the two bottles of wine he had had with his dinner and the new approachability of Lord Travis, swung about drunkenly.

"Ah, there y'are, Gallant. Just speakin' of you," he said with a leering sort of grin.

"Oh? I hope it was nothing actionable," quipped Travis good-naturedly.

"Depends, old fellow, depends," replied Mr. Johnstrow with a giggle. "Don't know if you'd actually set the law on your own cousin."

"Does anyone understand what he is talking about?" asked Travis, raising a quizzical eyebrow at the group of gentlemen.

"Tellin' you, ain't I? It's that book everyone's carryin' on about."

"What book is that?" Travis asked.

"Mean to say you haven't heard about it. Why, man, 's all 'bout you."

The forbidding brows began to draw together. "About me? Will someone explain what he is trying to say," asked Travis, looking about the group. No man there spoke or met his eye. He turned back to Mr. Johnstrow. "Pull yourself together, Johnstrow, and try to be a little more clear."

"It's that book—called something about a rake. It's been all anyone's talked about for a least a week or more. Good God, man, you must have heard about it. They say it's the story of your life. Never read it myself, 'course."

Travis said coldly, "And where, pray, does my cousin come into this? And which cousin? I have several."

"Why, Lady Brinton. She wrote it. My wife had it for a fact from Lady Bryn and she's related to Lady Brinton and should know."

Travis turned on his heel abruptly and left the room without another word. As he was leaving the club he met Burton just entering and turned back with him. "I must speak to you, Burton. Have you a moment?"

"All the evening, if you like. Come along into the library. Not likely to be in use at this time of night." He gestured to a passing servant and ordered a bottle of wine. They found the room deserted and settled before the fire. They did not speak until the wine had been served and the servant had departed.

"Well, my friend, it has been weeks since I have seen you looking so serious. What is wrong?"

"What do you know of some book about me?" rapped out Travis abruptly.

"Oh, Lord," sighed Burton. "So you've got onto that, have you?"

"You knew about it, then?"

"Well, very little else has been talked of since it came out."

"Why have I not heard of it?"

"I cannot think of anyone who would have the, er, hardihood to speak of it to your face."

"Not even you?"

"No," admitted his friend wryly. "I hoped it would be old news by now and there would be no need."

"But it is not old news. Why?"

"I am afraid that miserable Bryn woman has fanned the flames by putting it about that Georgeanne Brinton wrote it. I got onto Brinton at once and told him he'd best speak to Bryn, but clearly it had little effect. How did you hear of all this?''

''Johnstrow was kind enough to inform me just a few moments ago.''

''Ah, yes. Drunk, I take it?''

''Quite. He seemed knowledgeable about the business, though. Said he's had it from his wife, who is one of Caroline Bryn's cronies. Now, why would Caroline Bryn want to put about such a story of her own sister-in-law if it were not true.''

''Malice. She is not a nice woman. Good Lord, have you thought, Gallant? She will be your sister-in-law soon, won't she?''

Travis shuddered. ''Dreadful thought. However, she and Dilys are not at all close, so I doubt we will be forced much into her company. But that is by the way. Have you read this book?''

''No. I never read novels, you know, except for those of Miss Austen.''

''Could Georgeanne have written it, do you think?''

Burton shrugged. ''I should very much doubt it, but how could I possibly know such a thing?''

''Well, I shall know, no later than tomorrow morning,'' promised Travis, his dark brows drawn into a straight line of displeasure.

He would have liked very much to confront Georgeanne now, but the hour was much too late for a call. He had to content himself with a restless night that not even thoughts of Dilys could sweeten. He was convinced the story must be true, for who else but Georgeanne could have written a book purported to be the story of his life?

No amount of scandal about him had ever bothered him

in the least, but for Georgeanne to sit down and write a book about him and allow it to be published made him very angry indeed.

It was in a cold rage that he presented himself on the Brinton doorstep at nine the following morning and asked for a few words in private with Lady Brinton.

Georgeanne received this message while at breakfast. Harry had just left and Dilys was not yet down. She put down her cup of chocolate and went at once, thinking this must be something to do with the wedding arrangements.

"Dearest Travis, so early! Dilys is not down, but I will send word to her that you are here."

"Please do not. It is with you I must speak."

"Dear me, so very serious. What have I done now?"

"Well you may ask. What do you know of a book about me that is all the tittle-tattle now?"

"Oh, dear. I had hoped you would not get to hear of it."

"Why?"

"Why? Well, because, well, I knew you would not like it," she finished lamely.

"You read the book, then?"

"Oh, of course. Since everyone was going on so about it, I had to see what it was they were talking of. And really, Travis, it is nothing at all to—"

"Nothing? Nothing to have a book about oneself become the chief subject for all the worst gossips in town?"

"Please do not fly into the boughs, Travis. It is not a bad book; actually it—"

"I am not interested in its literary merits, though I suppose that would interest you!"

"Good Lord, no. I cannot claim that it has literary merits, I only—"

"Now you are being too modest, Georgeanne."

"Modest? I don't . . . What on earth do you mean?"

"I mean that, as its author you—"

"Author? What do you . . . I am not . . ." spluttered Georgeanne, genuinely bewildered, for the latest gossip had not reached her; and Harry, hoping it never would, now he had spoken to Alun, had not told her of his own knowledge.

"You stand there and declare to my face that you did not write this book?"

"Of course I did not wr—"

"Naturally you will deny it."

"Naturally I will," she snapped. "I cannot think why you should say such a thing."

"Oh, it is not just I who say it. Everyone says it. And they heard it first from Caroline Bryn. Why should your own sister-in-law say such a thing if it were not true?"

"But—but—I do not understand. How could she say such a thing? What can she possibly know about it?"

"Perhaps because it is true."

"It is not true. I did not write that book," cried Georgeanne angrily.

The drawing-room door opened on these words and Dilys stood there. She had come down to breakfast to learn that Lord Travis was in the house and had hurried along to the drawing room, her heart singing with gladness at the eagerness of her lover. The words she heard as she opened the door were like a pail of cold water in her face. Her happy smile faded and she looked apprehensively at Travis.

"What—what is it?" she whispered as an icy finger of foreboding seemed to draw itself up her spine.

"Please do not trouble yourself, my love. Just allow me a few more moments in private with Georgeanne," Travis said stiffly.

"But I . . . What is this about a—a book?"

"Dilys, this does not concern—" began Travis.

"Oh, don't be so starchy, Travis! Why make a mystery

of it to Dilys and cause her to be unhappy? We are all family here. It is that awful book everyone is talking about. Travis claims to have heard talk now that I wrote it.''

"I do not just claim it. I *have* heard it. Never would I have believed you could betray our friendship this way, Georgeanne. And then to deny it.''

"I did not write that book, Travis! For heaven's sake, what can I say to convince you? Why will you believe Caroline Bryn and not me? You have known me all your life and I have never lied to you, have I? I did not—'' Georgeanne's voice broke on a sob and she could not go on. She turned away as the tears flowed freely down her cheeks.

"Travis, you must stop teasing her. You have made her cry and I will not allow it,'' said Dilys, her face perfectly white and her mouth shaking. "Of course she did not write the book. I—I wrote it myself.''

They both turned blankly astounded faces upon her, and an awful moment of silence ensued. At last Travis said, "I think it is unnecessary for you to do this, Dilys. Georgeanne is perfectly capable of defending herself.''

"But she need not, for she is innocent of what you accuse her. I wrote that book when I was fifteen and still living at Caroline's. Just to—just to pass the time, really. I was always writing stories then. It kept me from—from being in low spirits and—and—'' her words faltered to a stop.

Travis was bending one of his looks upon her. The one she had always feared would shrivel her up entirely if he used it upon her. She could only wish that it would do so now, or that the floor would open and swallow her.

"You wrote this book about me?'' She nodded, unable to speak. "May I ask why?'' he demanded harshly.

"You were the only person I knew anything about, and then Caroline's friends were always gossiping about you— and I have known you all your life and Mademoiselle said—''

"You wrote it. And how did it come to be published?"

"I always sent my stories to Mademoiselle for, well, criticism. The girl she was governess to happened to read it and got her parents to read it and her father happened to be friends with a publisher and mentioned it to him. He, the publisher, wanted it and—and we—I—sold it to him. Oh, Travis, forgive me. I never thought—"

"No," he cut in gratingly, "I don't suppose you did!" Without another word or even a bow he left the room.

Dilys stood rooted, her face paper-white. Georgeanne went to her and put her arms about her shoulder. Slow tears welled up in Dilys' eyes and rolled unheeded down her cheeks. She patted Georgeanne's hand and drew away. She crossed the room slowly and went out. After the door closed behind her Georgeanne heard her dragging steps on the stairs as she went up to her room.

Georgeanne stood there, appalled at the dreadful scene just played out. She longed to follow her sister, be with her, but she knew Dilys required solitude at the moment. Only Travis could comfort her now, and there had been something so very final about the way he had left them. No, surely not final. He could not leave Dilys forever over such a silly thing as this. Could he?

In her room Dilys sat on the side of her bed, still crying soundlessly. She felt only a terrible coldness that seemed to radiate from the very marrow of her bones. It was fear. Fear that she had done something irrevocable and he would never forgive her for it. Fear that she had lost him, that he would never even want to see her again, much less marry her.

At last she felt in her pocket for her handkerchief and pulled out the crumpled letter from Mlle. she had picked up from the breakfast table and hurriedly thrust into her pocket when she had heard that Travis had called. She broke the seal and opened it. Through a blur of tears she read that

Mlle., having heard gossip that Georgeanne had written the book, had written to the publisher to request that he publish the news that she, Mlle., was the true author. This would, she hoped, silence all further talk and speculation.

Then Dilys at last felt her heart nearly burst with pain. She began to sob aloud as a little child does, for it was too late now. Far too late. Even though the talk might be stopped, Travis knew.

23

I have had no word from him for two days. I am trying to be brave and not subject everyone in the house to my unhappiness, but I think sometimes I shall lose my wits entirely and run about screaming out my pain and tearing my hair like a madwoman. I have forced myself to go down to dinner, but I cannot go out. I cannot. Wedding presents are pouring in at a greater rate than ever, but I will not look at them or even hear about them, since I am sure they will all have to be returned. Oh, dear God, what shall I do?

The tears came with this last sentence and Dilys was forced to put away her diary and get out her handkerchief again. There was a soft tap at the door and Georgeanne came in.

"I thought I heard . . . Oh, I did. Darling girl, you must not fret so. He will get over this. I refuse to believe that the Travis I know will ruin two lives out of a fit of pique."

"It seemed much more than a fit of pique, Georgie."

"That is just his way. It is those eyebrows! I am sure he will be in a bad temper for a few days and then cool down and come around to apologize."

"I wish I could feel so sanguine about it," Dilys said sadly.

"That is because you don't really know him as well as I do yet. All that adoration clouds your picture of him. By the way, Conklin, Burrows put a notice in the papers today stating that the author of the book is Mademoiselle Fleury."

"I knew they were to do so. She wrote to tell me she had

asked them to do it. She is so very good. But it is too late."

"Too late? Darling, you will see, in a day or so the whole thing will be forgotten. That I might have written it was food for gossip, but that some unknown governess wrote it is not interesting. She is very brave, bless her; it is just the sort of thing she would do. Harry has instructed his man of business to purchase an annuity for her. He says it is the least he can do."

"But I mean it is too late, since Travis already knows the truth."

"But he will never speak of it to a soul."

"No. Of course he will not, but he knows and despises me for having written it."

"Of course he does not despise you. Do not think such a thing, my darling," Georgeanne protested warmly, hugging Dilys to her protectively.

"Oh, if only I had never written the wretched thing!"

"Why did you, dearest? No, not why did you write it, because I think I understand that, but why did you sell it?"

"Oh, it sounds so stupid now that I know my true circumstances, but until you came home, Georgie, you know that I did not know—about the money, I mean. No one had ever explained it to me. Oh, of course I knew I would never starve, and that if I were in real need I could write to you, but . . . Well, I hated it so at Alun's house. And the life Miss Poore had then as an unmarried relative with no money at all horrified me. I began to think it might become my lot. Oh, please do not laugh at me!"

"Forgive me, darling. Please go on. What did you think?"

"That if I could become really good at it—writing, I mean—and could make money, I could move away with Miss Poore when I came of age and we could have a small house in the country or a set of rooms somewhere. Caroline would have had no objections to ridding herself of the pair of us, I assure you."

"Did Caroline know that you wrote those stories?"

"Oh, no! I would never have told her such a thing. Why?"

"Only that she, it seems, is the one who started the story that I was the author of your book. If she had known you wrote . . . Well, you see what I mean. It simply staggers me that she could have come up with my name. Indeed, why she should come up with anyone's name."

"Because she is truly evil, I believe. At least, she is very bad, and she adores to gossip. It is her favorite thing to do in all the world. That is where I learned so much about Travis' life. They could not stop talking about him."

"But I still cannot imagine what made her think of me."

"Something she picked up somewhere, I suppose. We shall probably never really know."

Two more days passed with no word from Travis, and Dilys sank into despair. The wedding was now but a week away. Her wedding clothes had all been delivered and were spread about in a spare bedroom, but she would not go to look at them.

Georgeanne, dressed for going out, came to Dilys' room hoping to tempt Dilys to come with her. She found her sister sitting on her chaise longue staring listlessly into space. "My dearest, I wish you would not do this to yourself. You will become ill if you do not eat more and take some air. Will you not come out driving with me today? People will begin to think the worst if they do not see you at all when the wedding is so near."

"There will be no wedding, I know that now. He is not going to forgive me."

"Nonsense. Now, do be sensible and come out for a drive with me."

"I cannot, Georgie. Truly I cannot."

"Very well, I won't tease you. I really came to tell you some good news about Miss Poore. She did not like to tell you herself when you are so unhappy."

"Sir Wicklow," breathed Dilys softly.

"Yes! Sir Wicklow! He has written proposing marriage to Miss Poore."

"Oh, Georgie, how truly wonderful! She will have him?"

"Indeed she will. I have never seen her look so radiant."

"I must go to her at once," Dilys declared.

"There's my good girl. Of course you must. She is in the back drawing room."

So Dilys went down to wish Miss Poore happy with a smile she had no need to force, so glad was she for this great good fortune come to the woman she had grown to love over their years together. Nevertheless, there were tears shed by both ladies, and for both they were made up of the sweet and the bitter.

Georgeanne, despite her bracing protestations that nothing so very serious had happened, was in truth beginning to worry a great deal. When she got into her carriage, she gave orders, on an impulse, to be driven to Travis' house. She would just say a few words about common sense and true love, and not lecture him about how unhappy he was making Dilys.

Travis' servant, however, said that his master was from home, so she was forced to climb back into her carriage and go away, though she was convinced he *was* at home. Sitting in there sulking and refusing all callers. It was frustrating, but she could hardly force her way into the house. She did some shopping and returned home to find Lady Sommers had just arrived.

After greetings were exchanged, Lady Sommers, with her usual bluntness, came straight to the point. "Since Dilys sent down word that she was confined to her bed with a sick headache, I can only assume that the rumors I have heard are true."

"Rumors! What rumors?" Georgeanne asked fearfully.

"That Dilys has been jilted."

"Oh, dear heaven! Of course she has not been jilted. How could such a rumor begin?"

"I can tell you that. A scullery maid of yours told her sister that 'miss' spends all day in her room crying and her trays come back untouched. The conclusion in the servants' hall is that 'miss' has lost her young man. The sister works for Mrs. Hay-Trenton, who is a close friend of Caroline Bryn's, who told it to a friend of mine and no doubt is making it her business to noise it abroad. Really, the woman should be put down as one would a mad dog! Now, please, let me have the word with no bark on it. I am not such a maggoty creature that I will have a heart attack if I hear the truth."

"There has been some unpleasantness," ventured Georgeanne cautiously.

"He has jilted her, then?"

"Oh, no, no! I . . . The truth is—"

"Yes, that would be the best thing," rapped out Lady Sommers.

Georgeanne thought for a moment. She saw no way out but to tell her aunt everything. At least she knew it would never be repeated to anyone, and she could hardly sit here and tell the woman lies. So Georgeanne told her aunt all about Caroline's bruiting it about that she, Georgeanne, had written the book about Travis, about Travis' confrontation, and Dilys' confession.

"And then he simply left and we haven't heard a word for four days now. I cannot believe he will not come to his senses eventually, but the wedding, as you know, is only a week away. And Dilys is too swamped by her misery and guilt to face anyone, and barely eats enough to keep alive. I am terribly worried. I tried to see him this morning, but he denied himself. What shall I do?"

"Do nothing. He would not listen to you in any case. But he will listen to me, or I will know the reason why. And

the sooner the better, it seems to me,'' Lady Sommers said
grimly, and rose to her feet.

"I wish you better luck than my own. I fear he will not
receive you.''

"Do not have any fears on that score, my dear.''

Lady Sommers had herself driven at once to Gallant House,
and there she too was informed that m'lord was from home.
"Then I will wait,'' said Lady Sommers, and marched past
the helpless butler and straight into the drawing room. "You
can bring me some wine and biscuits,'' she ordered grandly,
settling herself comfortably upon a sofa. The wine and
biscuits were brought and the butler dismissed. He was much
troubled. His master was shut up in the library, having left
strict orders not to be disturbed and not to admit any callers.
What if he should come out and the old lady see him? Should
he not warn his master?

A half-hour passed. The butler, after consultation with the
cook and head housemaid, returned to the drawing room to
inquire if Lady Sommers required any further service. He
found her very much at ease, sipping her wine and reading
from a book of sermons.

"No, no, nothing at all, thank you. I am quite comfortable.
I have nothing at all planned for this afternoon and would
as soon be here as anywhere.''

The butler again withdrew. Another half-hour passed. At
last the butler felt he had to take the matter in hand. The
old lady might stay the rest of the day! He tapped lightly
upon the library door and was told to "Go away,'' in no
uncertain terms. He quailed, but nevertheless he entered the
room.

"I told you not to disturb me,'' Travis growled.

"My lord, I do beg your pardon for going against your
express orders, but a situation has arisen and I felt I must
inform you of it.''

"All right. Just cut all the circumlocution and get to the point."

"It is Lady Sommers, sir. She is in the drawing room."

"How did she get there? Did I not say that I was out to all callers?"

"Yes, my lord, and so I told her. She just, well, came in and said she would wait. She has been here an hour now and I—"

"Oh, the devil take it! Very well. I will go to her."

He threw open the drawing-room door and said, "Well, what is it?" with a dreadful scowl.

"Ah, charming as always. Good afternoon, dear boy. I thought you would never come home. Will you join me in some wine?"

"No."

"You are such a gracious host, dear boy."

"I did not choose to be a host today, if I may remind you."

"Travis, I can only allow you so much discourtesy. Please to remember I am your relative and an elderly lady, and behave yourself. Now sit down and tell me what this is all about."

"I suppose Georgeanne sent you?"

"No one sent me. I am not the sort of person others can *send*. I please myself always. Now, I know there is some nonsense you've got in your head about this foolish book business. I want to know one thing. Have you read it?"

"Good God! You don't seriously think I would?"

"Well, I have read it and I think you should do so—and at once. Today. That is all I came to say to you, and believe me when I tell you that I have never given anyone a better piece of advice in my life. Good day to you, dear boy." With that she sailed past him and out of the room.

24

I am too low in spirits to write anything that does not sound dreary and will pull me down further still. Another day of silence. I know I have only myself to blame for everything that has happened, but I cannot prevent extremely bitter thoughts about Caroline. If she had not made up her lie about Georgeanne, none of this need ever have happened, for I know Travis would have cared nothing about the book, even if he had come to hear about it. It was only when he heard that Georgeanne had written it that he became angry. It is unChristian to wish that Caroline should suffer as I have these past days, and I hope I shall never sink to such a thing, but it is difficult, on the other hand, to wish her well.

Indeed, all was not well for Caroline. Constrained by fear for her husband's life, she found it difficult, nevertheless, to give up her conviction that it had been Georgeanne who had written the book, especially as she had felt herself so clever in figuring everything out. Apart from that, not only had there been no invitation of any sort from the Duchess of Portshire, but the woman had given her the cut direct in the park only yesterday when Caroline was out driving with Mrs. Johnstrow. Caroline knew her friend too well not to know that she would have news of that snub spread all over the town by now.

What she did not know was that her friend, in the days

before the Conklin, Burrows announcement came out in print, had done her work for her, and the town was abuzz with the news about Georgeanne and the book. Alun, his usual obtuseness pierced by fear for his life, seemed to hear Georgeanne's name everywhere he turned, and he expected at any moment to feel the clap of Harry's hand on his shoulder. He was so furious with his wife for having placed him in such a position that on the third day he ordered Caroline to be ready to leave for the country on the following morning, not only to punish her, but in order to be able to leave town himself. Harry would surely not follow him into the country with a challenge.

Caroline protested vehemently and at last resorted to tears, but he hardened his heart and refused to hear her. She at last gained the concession of two more days, citing her inability to pack and make ready four children for such an exodus in so short a time. Alun shut himself into his library and only came out for his dinner, to prevent any chance encounter with Harry, while Caroline turned the household upside down in her preparations.

Then the Conklin, Burrows announcement appeared in the papers and Caroline pleaded for a reprieve, saying there could be no danger to his life now. Alun, however, was finding some pleasure in his new assertion of mastery and refused to allow his spoken word to be trifled with. It was a new and gratifying feeling for him to have his word become law in his own house, and he was not prepared to give away what he had gained. He forcefully declared that they would leave for the country as he had dictated.

Just as Georgeanne had predicted, all talk of the book and its author had died abruptly with the publisher's announcement. The *ton* were now busily chewing over the details of the Earl of Pevely's wife, who had eloped with a footman in her husband's employ. There were several juicy bits to

this scandal. For instance, the couple had made their way
to Dover, there to embark for France, in the earl's own
coach, the footman driving. Then the wife had absconded
with all the Pevely family jewels, which had been handed
down for generations. And best of all, the countess had been
five months pregnant and there were titillating discussions
about whose child it was she carried.

Caroline missed most of this, being too much occupied
to go out or to receive callers, but on the last day before
departure she ordered the carriage to take her to the shops
for things she felt she could not leave London without, and
it was in the Burlington Arcade that she came face to face
with Georgeanne, strolling along arm in arm with the
Duchess of Portshire.

Caroline's face was a study as she beheld them, her feelings
a mixture of ire, envy, and what could only be described
as betrayal to find her arch enemy so intimate with the height
of Caroline's social amibitions. By whom or in what way
she felt betrayed, she could not have explained, only that
she did not want to believe it could be so. For some reason
Caroline had felt the duchess her own preserve and she could
not bear that even here Georgeanne had trumped her ace.
That Caroline held no ace so far as the duchess was con-
cerned, made no difference to Caroline. She had not yet given
up hope, despite the snubbing she had received in the park,
that she could win the duchess over.

So, despite her fury with Georgeanne, she swallowed her
pride and forced herself onward, smiling ingratiatingly, to
greet them. Alas, even as she approached she heard the
duchess say, ''If you will excuse me for just a few moments,
my dear, I must just step in here and pick up some gloves
I have ordered.'' She turned away with a pretense of not
having noticed Caroline's approach, and Georgeanne, understanding her motive, stood to await Caroline. She seemed

not to see Caroline's outstretched hand. "Good morning, Caroline," she said coldly.

Caroline looked distractedly after the duchess, as though she might follow her into the store, but then apparently thought better of it. "Good morning, dear Georgeanne. I hope I see you well?"

"Very well."

"Oh, I am so glad. And dear Dilys?"

"She is very well also."

"How happy you make me. I was so afraid—well, I had heard the most distressing rumors."

"*Heard*?" said Georgeanne, loading the word with sarcastic disbelief, for she knew who had started the rumors about Travis and Dilys.

Caroline colored and bridled defensively, but knew better than to cross swords with Georgeanne on this subject. She bared her teeth in a stiff smile. "So the wedding is next week! How sorry we are to miss it, but Alun insists on taking the children out of London for their health."

"For his health, do you say?" asked Georgeanne mischievously, having by now heard from Harry of his encounter with Alun.

"No! For the children's health, I said," retorted Caroline angrily.

"Ah, I felt sure I had misheard, for since the Conklin, Burrows announcement, I was sure Alun would be feeling much better."

"What are you implying? How dare you insinuate . . . Why should my husband care for that?"

"Why, surely it must be a relief to him to have someone so closely related to him cleared of suspicion," Georgeanne said suavely.

"Oh, well, as to that—" stuttered Caroline, the wind so completely taken out of her sails she could think of no pertinent rejoinder. She gnashed her teeth in fury. Why did this woman always manage to make her feel a fool?

Georgeanne had had enough of Caroline. "Well, I must bid you good-bye now or my dear friend will think I have abandoned her." She turned away before Caroline could speak, but then turned back to fire her parting shot. "Oh, by the way, I am sure you will rejoice, as we all do, at the news that our dear Miss Poore is soon to become the wife of Sir Wicklow Pryce." With that she retired into the shop in triumph, for Caroline's reaction had been all that she could have wished.

"She sort of swelled up and turned almost purple. I truly thought she might burst with rage," Georgeanne reported to Dilys later in the day.

"Oh, I wish I might have seen her face," said Dilys, with her first smile for days at the thought of Caroline's discomfiture.

"It was a treat. You would also have liked to see it when she saw me with Hermione. If she had had a dagger in her hand, I would not answer for it but that she would have run me through. And Hermione cut her again. Oh, it was altogether lovely and pays her out for all her wickedness. They are leaving for the country in the morning, you know. I am sure it is because Harry let Alun think he would call him out if he did not stop Caroline from spreading those rumors."

"But since then the announcement about Mademoiselle has come out. I wonder why they persist in going. Caroline hates the country."

"Perhaps Alun is afraid Harry will think that he was going only because he was frightened, and if he changes his mind now, Harry will think he was a coward running from a fight."

"Would Harry really have called him out?"

"Good Lord, no. He only meant to move him to do something about Caroline. Well, we are well rid of them."

"I wish I were going."

"What? With Caroline and Alun?"

"No, of course not. But out of London."

"You cannot leave before your wedding, darling. After that you will be away from London long enough."

"Oh, Georgie," Dilys said with an unhappy sigh.

On that same day, as she inspected the fawn silk gown she had ordered made especially for Dilys' wedding, Mlle. was brought news by Miss Threese.

"You will never guess what has happened, Mademoiselle. You may never get the chance to wear that gown," said the impudent Miss Threese.

"You must learn to knock before entering anyone's room other than your own, Mademoiselle Threese," replied Mlle. severely.

"Oh, I knew you would not truly mind," replied Miss Threese carelessly. "Don't you want to hear my news?"

"Is this more gossip from school? I sometimes wonder how the young ladies there find the time to do their lessons when they spend so much time with their heads together spreading slander."

"Oh, lessons are such a waste of time, really."

"Then you should inform your father so and relieve him of the burden of such an expense."

"Oh, Mademoiselle, don't be so starchy or I shall not tell you the news I have heard about Miss Bryn."

Mlle. could not prevent herself from starting at the name. "What of Miss Bryn?"

Miss Threese giggled. "There now! I knew that would make you take notice and stop scolding. She has been jilted, that is what!"

"That is an absurdity. The wedding is but a week away. Really, people will say anything to make themselves important."

"But it is true. Everyone is talking of it. She has not been seen for five days now and has sent regrets for all parties, even those in her honor, and they say she has not eaten a morsel of food in all this time and stays locked in her room crying," finished Miss Threese breathlessly.

"Miss Threese, these are all made-up details. Since she has not been seen, there is no one who could know what she does in the privacy of her family, and you may be sure none of them would spread such tales. To gossip is evil, to spread gossip is just as bad. It is beneath the dignity of a gentlewoman to participate in either. If you have any pretensions to attain that state you will take my advice and spurn taking any part in it. Now, I am very busy."

Miss Threese went meekly away at this dismissal, her whole body feeling scorched by such a scolding. Mlle. immediately put on her bonnet and went to call upon Georgeanne. She was received with open arms, as always. The children were sent for and made their bows, little Daisy was examined and admired, and Harry's health was minutely inquired into.

"And now, Lady Brinton, what of Mademoiselle Dilys?" asked Mlle. when they were again alone together.

"Oh, how remiss of me. I will send word to her that you are here."

"Please do not, just at present. I have heard a most distressing and, I pray, untrue story of some trouble. Is it possible for you reassure me as to its falseness?"

Then for the second time Georgeanne felt it necessary to tell this good friend the sad story. Mlle. listened in grim silence, then said, "It surely cannot be so that the Lord Travis will abandon her over such a trifle as that."

"I had not thought it possible, but now . . . Well, he has not come or sent word for five days."

"He will," said Mlle. forcefully. "He is too much the

gentleman to behave badly in the end. He is the little boy sulking now. It was always so with him as a child, if you remember.''

Georgeanne said that she did remember and hoped very much all would still be well.

Mlle. rose to go, declining to see Dilys today. ''It will cause her sadness to see me, who is so very much responsible for her unhappiness now. I should never have allowed the book to be sold.''

When Mlle. reached her own room again, she went straight to her desk and sat silently for a time, gathering her thoughts. Then she reached for her pen and wrote:

> My dear Lord Travis Gallant,
>
> I believe you will perhaps remember Mademoiselle Fleury, who was Lady Brinton's governess so many years. I hope you will not think it presumptuous of me to address you thus, but I felt it my duty to say a few words to you about the book written by Mademoiselle Dilys Bryn.
>
> We were separated when Lord and Lady Langthorne died, but we continued to correspond and I encouraged her to write stories because she was so very much alone and desolate, and not treated with sympathy in her brother's home. Writing was a means for her to escape from her wretchedness. The book that so unfortunately came to be printed through my auspices, was written with love, as I think you will find if you will but read it. Indeed, that love has been the mainstay of her life from the time she was nine years old.
>
> Please forgive me if I seem interfering, but believe that I mean only the best for your happiness, my dear sir, and remain,
>
> Your very good friend,
> Hortense Fleury

25

I shall not keep this diary anymore. I will close it up and put it away forever. Or at least until I am too old to be moved by any emotions and only care that my chair is close to the fire and well out of drafts. I doubt I will ever write anything anymore, for the very act of writing will rouse too painful memories.

As Dilys wrote this, Travis sat in his study with her book in his lap and Mlle.'s letter in his hand.

After his Aunt Sommers' brief visit, he had sent a footman out to buy the book. It had not taken her pithy words to show him that he was behaving in an unmanly way. He was aware that he was sulking like a bear in its cave, but he was not aware of the pain he was causing Dilys by doing so. Georgeanne had only laughed at him when he behaved so when they were playfellows, and when he at last became bored by his own company and rejoined her, they went on as before as though nothing out of the way had happened. That Georgeanne was of a very different temperament than Dilys did not occur to him. He had not stopped loving her and had no idea of giving her up, but he was punishing her and knew it was childish of him. But despite this peripheral awareness, he had not yet been quite able to throw off his mood.

He had been truly angry first with Georgeanne when he had thought her the culprit, and then with Dilys when she had confessed. In both cases it had seemed a betrayal of friendship and his anger justified, but now he was beginning to feel uneasily that he had perhaps allowed his pride to have too much its own way with him. He too remembered similar episodes in his childhood and knew that his lack of years might have excused him then. But now?

These were the thoughts he had been brooding over when his Aunt Sommers had called, and his guilt had caused him to be rude to her. When she was gone, there was more guilt at treating her so, and this in turn had made him angry and tending to cast upon her the blame for his rudeness, for if she had not come interfering, he should not have been put in the position of behaving badly.

The illogic of this thinking had also obtained in his feelings toward Dilys and had held him in thrall these last few days. She had created this situation and therefore was to blame for his treatment of her, which he hated in himself.

He could not, however, remain comfortable with this version of events for long. He was a clear-thinking man generally, and knew he was now being unreasonable. He loved her very much and longed for her company. As in the old days, the punishment turned in upon himself if carried on too long.

He had sent for the book and had sat up most of the night reading it, finally falling asleep in his chair before the fire in the library. He started awake when the housemaid came in to clean out the grate and lay a fresh fire. She let out a shriek when she saw him and ran from the room.

In a moment his valet was there, much alarmed. "My lord! What is this? Are you ill? Why have you not slept in your bed?"

"Never mind. I will have a bath now. Make it ready at once, and I will come up."

"Very well, my lord," said the valet stiffly, offended not to be taken into his master's confidence.

After his bath Travis sat down and ate a large beefsteak for his breakfast, for he too had had little appetite these last few days. Then he dressed and went back to his library. He picked up Dilys' book and studied it. He had found it just such a trifle as the *ton* enjoyed, a *roman à clef* with easily identifiable characters. His own, or the one purported to be based upon himself, he did not recognize as himself at all. The character was written of so romantically, so sympathetically, that to Travis it was unrecognizable. Even the rake's worst peccadilloes were treated as evils arising out of wrongs done to him by others, which he, in honor and pride, refused to deny.

While he was musing thus, Mlle.'s letter was brought to him, and when he had read it, he knew exactly what she implied and agreed to its truth. He called for his carriage.

Meanwhile, Dilys had laid her diary away at the back of a bureau drawer. She dressed herself bravely in a new almond green cambric muslin gown and made her way downstairs with a determinedly cheerful expression on her face. She had resolved that nothing more was to be gained from moping and hiding but misery for her family. She must put all this behind her and return to her state of mind before Travis' proposal. Then she had known her love to be hopeless and herself fated for spinsterhood, as she could not imagine loving anyone else after his long reign over her heart. What had happened was only an interlude, a dream, and must be forgotten, for she could not allow herself to become a burden upon the happiness of all those she loved. She was fortunate to have a warm, enfolding family and knew very well that Georgeanne would never leave her alone in England. When they returned to India, she would travel with them. It would be a whole new life, one far away from anything she had ever known, and in time her pain would ease. She was not too young to recognize this truth, having suffered and recovered from the deaths of the Langthornes, the only parents she had ever known.

Georgeanne could guess from her sister's face most of what she was attempting to do now, and silently called Travis some very unladylike names. Really, the man was a monstrous baby! To stay away all these days, putting this child through so much torment. Georgeanne believed he was only repeating his old habit of withdrawing himself from one who had displeased him or injured his dignity and would reappear at any moment. But if it was so that he could not forgive Dilys and could not bring himself to come and tell her so, then he should at least write and tell her and end this dreadful suspense. She resolved that when Harry came home, she would ask him to call upon Travis and ask him his intentions.

Now she said, "Darling, I do think that gown turned out well. The color is so becoming to you."

"Yes, it is lovely. Thank you, Georgie," said Dilys with a smile that nearly broke Georgeanne's heart.

Miss Poore was seated with Georgeanne in the back drawing room and had been trying her best, while not absolutely condemning Lord Travis, to understand how so fine a gentleman could behave in so cruel a way to dear Dilys. Of course, they had called him a rake and he had created much scandal, but she knew those days were over since he had fallen in love with Dilys. How she could be so sure of this she could not have said, but she knew it was so.

Now she studied the pathetic and awful smile and wanted to weep at the gallantry of spirit it expressed. She also was distressed by the thin paleness of Dilys' face, into which the gray eyes seemed to have sunk somewhat and lost their brilliance, while at the same time seeming to have enlarged themselves and taken over the face entirely. There could be no doubt the past five days had taken their toll on her health and good looks.

"Dilys, my child," said Miss Poore, "could I not persuade you to come out for a walk with me?"

"Oh, no, I—" Then Dilys reminded herself sternly of her new resolution. "How kind of you. That will be lovely—only perhaps we might postpone it until later—in the day, I mean."

"Whenever it will please you, my dear," said Miss Poore mildly, though much elated at her success. "I am sure the air will bring back roses to those cheeks. London during the Season can be so debilitating."

"Well, it will soon be over and then we may all remove to the country. The boys are already so wild to go that I have been thinking of sending them ahead with Nanny."

"Oh, Georgie, do let me go with them to help," begged Dilys fervently.

Georgeanne only smiled and changed the subject, though determined in her mind that if Travis remained obdurate in this matter they would all leave at once for Plynton Abbey, the Brinton family seat. "Have you and Sir Wicklow settled upon a date yet, Miss Poore?"

Now, of course, all this had already been discussed and settled between Georgeanne and Miss Poore, but they went into the subject very thoroughly to divert Dilys, who did her best to assist their efforts by trying to join the conversation with a show of interest.

"We have thought at first here in London, but now . . . Oh, Dilys, Lady Brinton has insisted so kindly that I be married from Plynton Abbey. Of course, Sir Wicklow is delighted by this idea, as his own home is so nearby and we can be married in his own church by his own vicar."

"How perfect! Really, Georgie, you have a way of always hitting on just the right thing," said Dilys, wondering how she could bear up under the demands of this joyous occasion at a time she had expected to be on her own honeymoon in Europe. A month each in Paris, Rome, Florence, he had insisted upon, before going to Vienna and Switzerland, though saying they would not be bound by any special schedule, staying longer where it pleased them to do so. She shook her head to rid herself of these thoughts, which could not help her now.

". . . and then we shall just slip away quite quietly to Paris for a few weeks," Miss Poore was continuing. "Sir Wicklow does not like traveling a great deal and then we are past the age for long, romantic honeymoons." And then she could have bitten her tongue out in vexation at her words, sure they could only cause pain to Dilys.

A footman entered then with word that Lord Travis Gallant had called and would like to speak to Miss Bryn.

The three women sat for a stunned moment, unable to speak. Then Georgeanne and Miss Poore turned to Dilys, who seemed to turn even paler, if that were possible. She sat rooted and unresponsive in any other way.

Georgeanne rose and went to her. "Darling, Travis is here at last. Will you go to him?"

Dilys turned frightened, beseeching eyes up to her. "I don't believe I can."

"No, of course you need not. I think it will be better if Miss Poore and I slip away up the back stairs and have him sent in here to you. Just sit where you are, my own love."

This plan was followed at once, and then Dilys was alone, her heart pounding in a most unpleasant way, for surely he had come to ask for his release. He could not still love her after these five days of silence. They spoke his feelings clearly. And how was she to bear it without breaking down before him? Oh, he should have written to ask, indeed he should.

Travis was invited by the footman to step into the back drawing room, where he would find Miss Bryn waiting to receive him. He walked quickly down the hall and flung open the door. Dilys sat there, her eyes huge and . . . frightened? Yes, frightened! And did she really cower back in her chair when he appeared? Why was she so pale? Oh, heaven, what had he done?

"Dilys—dear God—can you forgive me?"

She seemed not to understand his words, for she only stared at him uncomprehendingly.

He crossed to her rapidly and flung himself on his knees before her. "My darling, my own dearest girl, I have made you suffer. I am truly the worst brute in the world not to have realized. I was being so selfish and you thought . . . Oh, Dilys, will you ever be able to forgive me?"

"But—but I do not . . . It is I who . . . Have you forgiven me?"

He took her hands and buried his face in them. "Ah, don't, please don't, my own, if you love me."

"Then—then you are not angry with me anymore?"

"Angry? Only with myself. How could I have . . . I do love you so very much, Dilys."

"Ah, Travis," she cried, her eyes bright with tears as his words finally came through to her bewildered senses.

He stood up and pulled her up into his arms hungrily. "Come, let me hold you. I have missed you so."

They stood for a long while locked together, each comforting themselves by the warmth of their embrace. Then she drew back to look up into his face for reassurance that his long absence had truly changed nothing, and he slowly bent his mouth down to hers and with small kisses from one side to the other reassured himself that those so well-remembered lips were as they had been. He at last seemed satisfied that they were, and he drew her even closer and went at the business more thoroughly.

This, of course, lasted for some little while as there were so many kisses to be made up for, but when at last they could bear to stop, they sat down together on the sofa, she snugly within the circle of his arms.

"I cannot believe I got up this morning wishing I might simply die, and now I wish I may never do so that I might have you forever," she said with a trembling sigh.

"You will have me forever if you can bear my stupidity," he said.

"Oh, do not say such a thing of yourself. You are not stupid. You had every right to be angry with me."

"But not to behave so childishly. I hope with your help never to behave so again. I promise I will try, at any rate, and if I relapse, you are to scold me roundly and remind me of this week when I made you so unhappy by my behavior."

"And I will promise never to write another book!"

"Well, at least not another about me. Besides, I have plans to keep you so busy for the next twenty years or so that you won't have any time left over for writing books. We shall be away nearly a year on our wedding trip, you know, and then I expect we will be starting our nursery."

She blushed and hid her face in his shoulder, but he pried it out and kissed her soundly. "Don't be missish," he said.

"No, Travis, I will not be. I am never so, really. Yes. Our nursery. You will want an heir," she said bravely.

"Eventually. But I shall be most satisfied first if it is a little minx of a girl with great bright-gray eyes and an inclination to say just what she thinks and never afraid to give anyone a set-down when deserved."

This statement was so satisfactory that she threw her arms about his neck and covered his face with kisses. He was more than content to allow himself to be adored.

Miss Poore and Georgeanne had all this time been sitting in unbearable suspense in Georgeanne's dressing room, and had finally been drawn downstairs. They hovered in the hallway, their eyes upon the closed door of the back drawing room.

"It is quite quiet," Miss Poore said, "no raised angry voices at all. That is a good sign, is not it?"

"A very good sign," declared Georgeanne. "I think we may be assured that all is well."

"Oh, I pray it may be so. Oh, dear, I fear I am going to cry."

"I must say I feel somewhat weepy myself. Come, let us go into the drawing room and wait for them to remember the world."

"You do not think . . . I mean, they have been alone there for so long. Is it quite proper? Should you not—"

Georgeanne laughed and, linking her arm through Miss Poore's, walked toward the drawing room. "Never in the world would I be such a spoilsport as that, Miss Poore."